Children's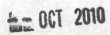
Rock Islan
401 - 19th Street
Rock Island, IL 61201-8143

OCT 2010

TWISTED JOURNEYS® #16

THE QUEST FOR DRAGON MOUNTAIN

ROBIN MAYHALL

ILLUSTRATED BY ALITHA E. MARTINEZ

GRAPHIC UNIVERSE™ · MINNEAPOLIS · NEW YORK

Story by Robin Mayhall

Pencils and inks by Alitha E. Martinez

Coloring by Hi-Fi Design

Lettering by Marshall Dillon

Copyright © 2010 by Lerner Publishing Group, Inc.

Graphic Universe™ is a trademark and Twisted Journeys® is a registered trademark of Lerner Publishing Group, Inc.

All rights reserved. International copyright secured. No part of this book may be reproduced, stored in a retrieval system, or transmitted in any form or by any means—electronic, mechanical, photocopying, recording, or otherwise—without the prior written permission of Lerner Publishing Group, Inc., except for the inclusion of brief quotations in an acknowledged review.

Graphic Universe™
A division of Lerner Publishing Group, Inc.
241 First Avenue North
Minneapolis, MN 55401 U.S.A.

Website address: www.lernerbooks.com

Library of Congress Cataloging-in-Publication Data

Mayhall, Robin.
    The quest for dragon mountain / by Robin Mayhall ; illustrated by Alitha E. Martinez.
        p.   cm. — (Twisted journeys)
    Summary: As the dragon-hero of this story, the reader is asked to make choices that determine the outcome of the tale.
        ISBN: 978–0–8225–9261–7 (lib. bdg. : alk. paper)
        1. Plot-your-own stories. 2. Graphic novels. [1. Graphic novels.
    2. Dragons—Fiction. 3. Plot-your-own stories.] I. Martinez, Alitha E., ill.
    II. Title.
    PZ7.7.M39Qu 2010
    [Fic]—dc22   2009032259

Manufactured in the United States of America
1 – DP – 7/15/10

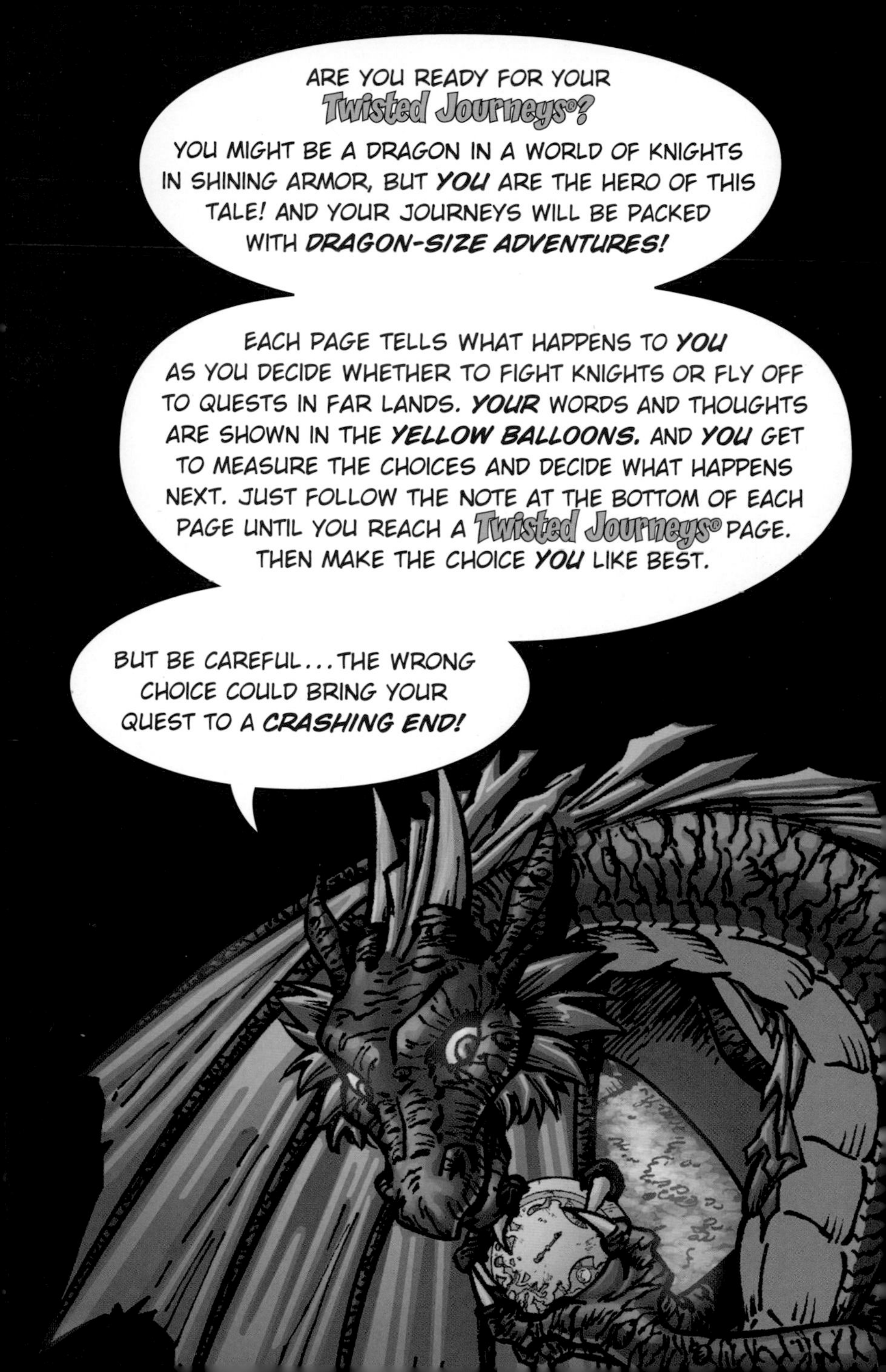
ARE YOU READY FOR YOUR Twisted Journeys®?
YOU MIGHT BE A DRAGON IN A WORLD OF KNIGHTS IN SHINING ARMOR, BUT YOU ARE THE HERO OF THIS TALE! AND YOUR JOURNEYS WILL BE PACKED WITH DRAGON-SIZE ADVENTURES!
EACH PAGE TELLS WHAT HAPPENS TO YOU AS YOU DECIDE WHETHER TO FIGHT KNIGHTS OR FLY OFF TO QUESTS IN FAR LANDS. YOUR WORDS AND THOUGHTS ARE SHOWN IN THE YELLOW BALLOONS. AND YOU GET TO MEASURE THE CHOICES AND DECIDE WHAT HAPPENS NEXT. JUST FOLLOW THE NOTE AT THE BOTTOM OF EACH PAGE UNTIL YOU REACH A Twisted Journeys® PAGE. THEN MAKE THE CHOICE YOU LIKE BEST.
BUT BE CAREFUL... THE WRONG CHOICE COULD BRING YOUR QUEST TO A CRASHING END!

Clink. Clink-clink.
Clink-clink-clinketyclinketyclinkety-CRASH!

The happy sound of a few golden coins clinking together turns into a loud metallic *crash!* as you roll over, half-asleep. Instead of taking a nice stretch, you slide down the side of a large pile of treasure. Your tail whips back and forth as you wave your clawed forelegs.

You try to grab something to stop your fall, but the coins and jewels just slide down with you. You end up flat on your back near the bottom of your hoard as a shower of coins rains down onto your scaly belly.

What a way to start your birthday! A wisp of smoke curls from your nostrils. But it's only smoke—no real heat or fire. You stayed up until midnight, hoping that would change on your birthday.

One whole year older, and nothing is different.

GO ON TO THE NEXT PAGE.

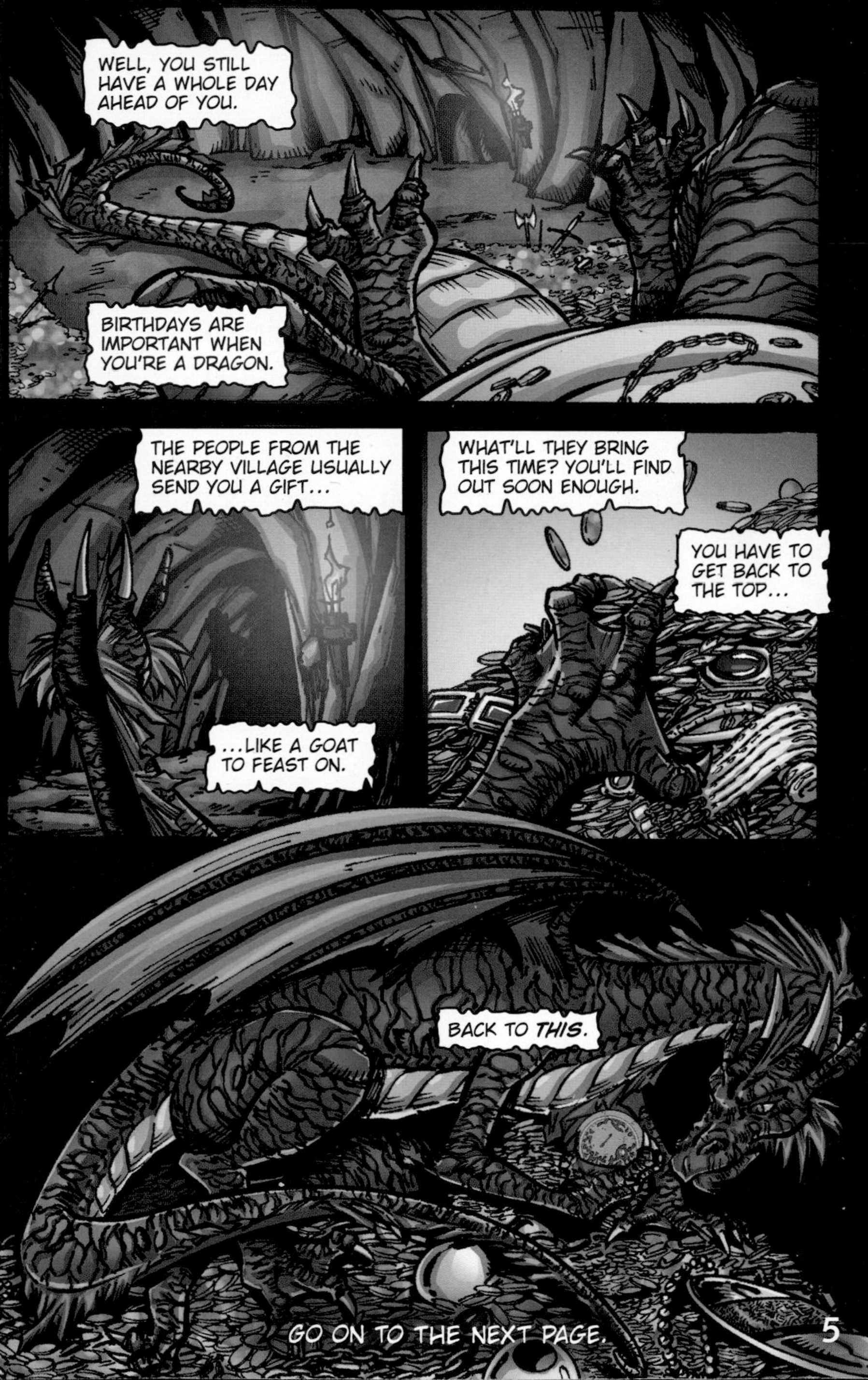
WELL, YOU STILL HAVE A WHOLE DAY AHEAD OF YOU.
BIRTHDAYS ARE IMPORTANT WHEN YOU'RE A DRAGON.
THE PEOPLE FROM THE NEARBY VILLAGE USUALLY SEND YOU A GIFT...
...LIKE A GOAT TO FEAST ON.
WHAT'LL THEY BRING THIS TIME? YOU'LL FIND OUT SOON ENOUGH.
YOU HAVE TO GET BACK TO THE TOP...
BACK TO *THIS*.

GO ON TO THE NEXT PAGE.

The dragons in your family have been collecting riches for hundreds of years, fighting knights and even other dragons to win the finest treasures. This is the most precious object in all your hoard.

It is an ancient clock, made far away and years ago. You've never seen anything else like it. The humans who live nearby sometimes use candles to tell time. When the candle burns down an inch, they know about an hour has passed. But mostly they don't worry about what time of day it is at all, other than "morning," "lunchtime," and "dinnertime." Only dragons want to keep track of hours, days, and even centuries.

Your clock is made of gold, with a face of pearls and diamonds. The hands are cut from emeralds. Inside is a set of bells that makes beautiful music. Whoever built this timepiece must have been a great artist . . . or even a magician.

Suddenly the clock begins to chime. *Oh, it's time already*, you think. The villagers come every year on your birthday.

GO ON TO THE NEXT PAGE.

You hear noises from the entrance to your lair. Someone is coming in through the narrow, rocky tunnel that leads outside.

WILL YOU . . .

. . . hold the clock safe in your claws and wait to see who enters?
TURN TO PAGE 18.

. . . hide the clock and hurry down to confront the villagers?
TURN TO PAGE 54.

The cliffs seem to call to you. The rocks here have different shapes and colors from the ones in your mountain lair. But the caves look like cozy places to live.

And there are a *lot* of caves! As you glide along over the beach, the ocean waves *whoosh* and *crash* below you. On one side of you is the cliff wall, dotted with cave entrances. Some caves are all the way down at sea level. Others are high up off the ground.

This would be a perfect place for dragons to live.

GO ON TO THE NEXT PAGE.

There could be dozens, even *hundreds*
of dragons here!

WILL YOU . . .

. . . yell out in the hope someone hears you?
TURN TO PAGE 104.

. . . peek quickly in each cave one by one?
TURN TO PAGE 74.

. . . cautiously choose one cave and
search it thoroughly?
TURN TO PAGE 31.

Although the knight looks strong and ready to fight, you decide to face him. You don't want to risk him or anyone else getting inside your cave and stealing your treasure. Or your wonderful clock.

As you think of your special clock and of how you're a whole year bigger and stronger than on your *last* birthday, you start to feel warm inside. In fact, you feel hot. It's like something is burning deep in your chest. First, a few wisps, then thick white clouds of smoke puff from your nostrils as you bare your teeth at the knight.

10

GO ON TO THE NEXT PAGE.

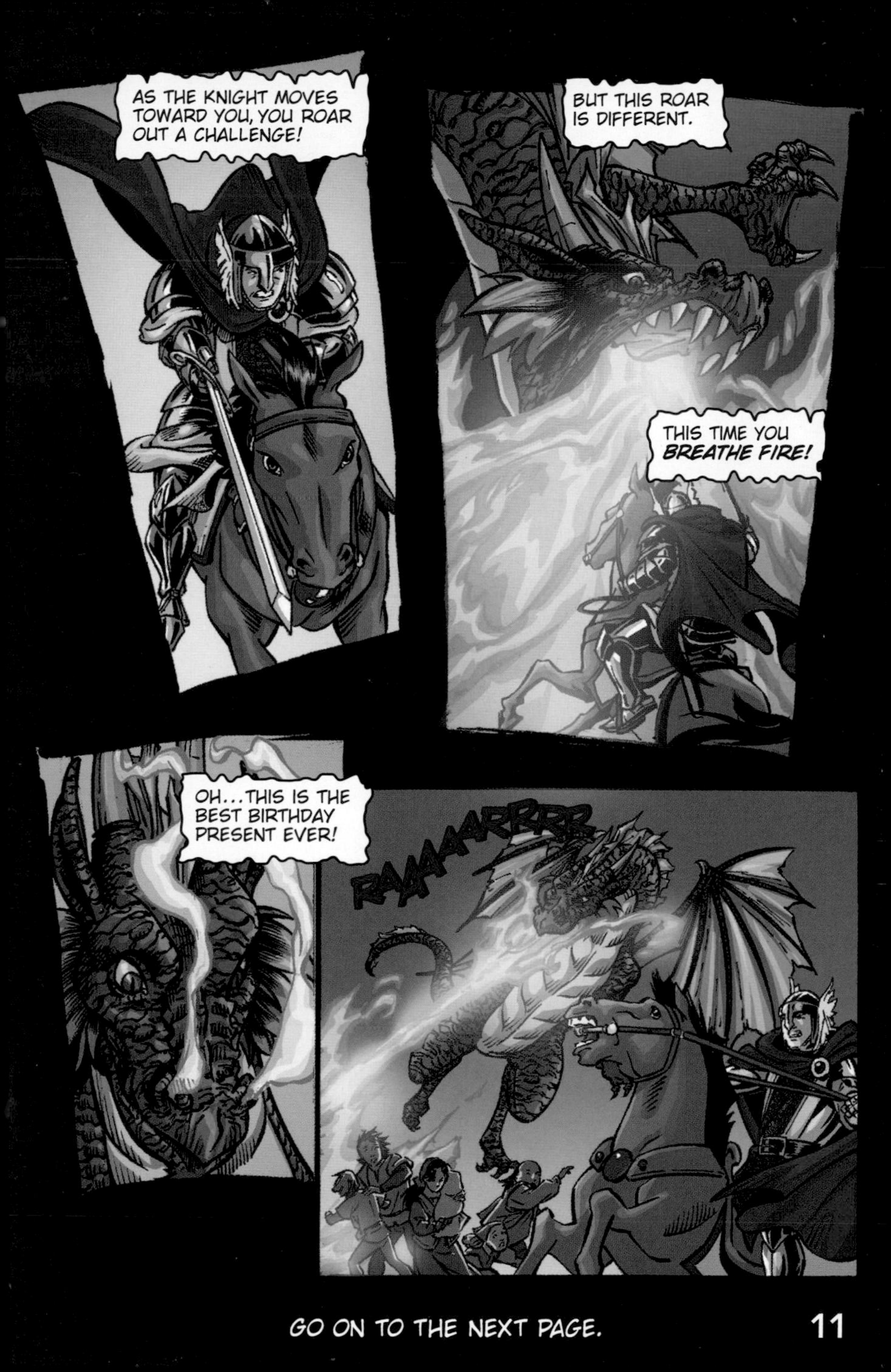
AS THE KNIGHT MOVES TOWARD YOU, YOU ROAR OUT A CHALLENGE!
BUT THIS ROAR IS DIFFERENT.
THIS TIME YOU *BREATHE FIRE!*
OH...THIS IS THE BEST BIRTHDAY PRESENT EVER!
RAAAAARRRRR

GO ON TO THE NEXT PAGE.

The villagers and even the knight run from you as fast as they can.

WILL YOU . . .

. . . chase after them for more fun?
TURN TO PAGE 40.

. . . go back to your cave to experiment with your new power?
TURN TO PAGE 94.

. . . try to find someone who can help you grow stronger?
TURN TO PAGE 22.

You block the entrance to your cave with piles of heavy shields and weapons from your hoard. But the knight seems determined. You hear more clanking sounds. Then the tip of the knight's sword pushes through a small hole in the pile of treasure.

You roar loudly and shove the pile hard, pushing it farther into the tunnel. As the echoes die away, you listen for the knight.

GO ON TO THE NEXT PAGE.

You wait and wait, but you hear nothing.

WILL YOU . . .

. . . assume the worst is over and
go rest on top of your hoard?
TURN TO PAGE 25.

. . . move the barricade and
peek down the tunnel?
TURN TO PAGE 102.

You throw caution to the wind and take another deep breath. Holding your clock up in one clawed hand, you let out a short flare of fire. The flames wrap around the clock and your claws, but neither seems hurt.

You look over your clock again carefully. As you are holding it close to your face again, it suddenly begins to chime, startling you. The song is different from either the birthday song or the hourly chime. But somehow, that makes sense. You are different now too.

The tune is very beautiful. You close your eyes and feel warm deep down inside. It must be a special song for a special birthday . . . and this *definitely* was a most special birthday. You look forward to a whole year of playing with your clock and your new talent.

THE END

You're tired of being tricked. You decide to have your meal of village girl. With a few shakes of your head, you smash the hut into a pile of branches, sticks, and straw. The girl starts to run away, but her grandmother stands her ground.

With a snap of your jaws, you gobble up the girl. The old woman is not smiling anymore. Her voice sounds strong and fearless as she says, "Now you will never know your true heritage!"

GO ON TO THE NEXT PAGE.

YOU CONSIDER GOBBLING UP THE OLD WOMAN TOO.

BUT YOUR STOMACH IS FULL...AND YOU'RE READY FOR A NAP.

SO YOU SETTLE FOR FLATTENING WHAT'S LEFT OF HER HUT.

FINALLY, THE LONGEST BIRTHDAY OF YOUR LIFE IS OVER.

YOU RETURN TO YOUR LAIR...

...AND YOUR TREASURE.

WHO NEEDS THOSE VILLAGERS, ANYWAY?

The End

You make yourself more comfortable on your bed—the deep pile of coins at the very top of your hoard. You turn the clock over in your claws while you wait to see who or what will come in through the tunnel.

At first the sounds are familiar. You hear hoofs clattering on rock. That means the villagers sent you a sacrifice. Then a loud *bleat* cuts through all other noises. The villagers shout as they herd a goat into the tunnel.

Over the sounds of the frightened goat, you hear

something else. Your hearing is very sharp. You can hear what sounds like a young girl crying.

Finally, a village girl comes out of the tunnel, leading a shaggy white goat by a short piece of rope.

GO ON TO THE NEXT PAGE.

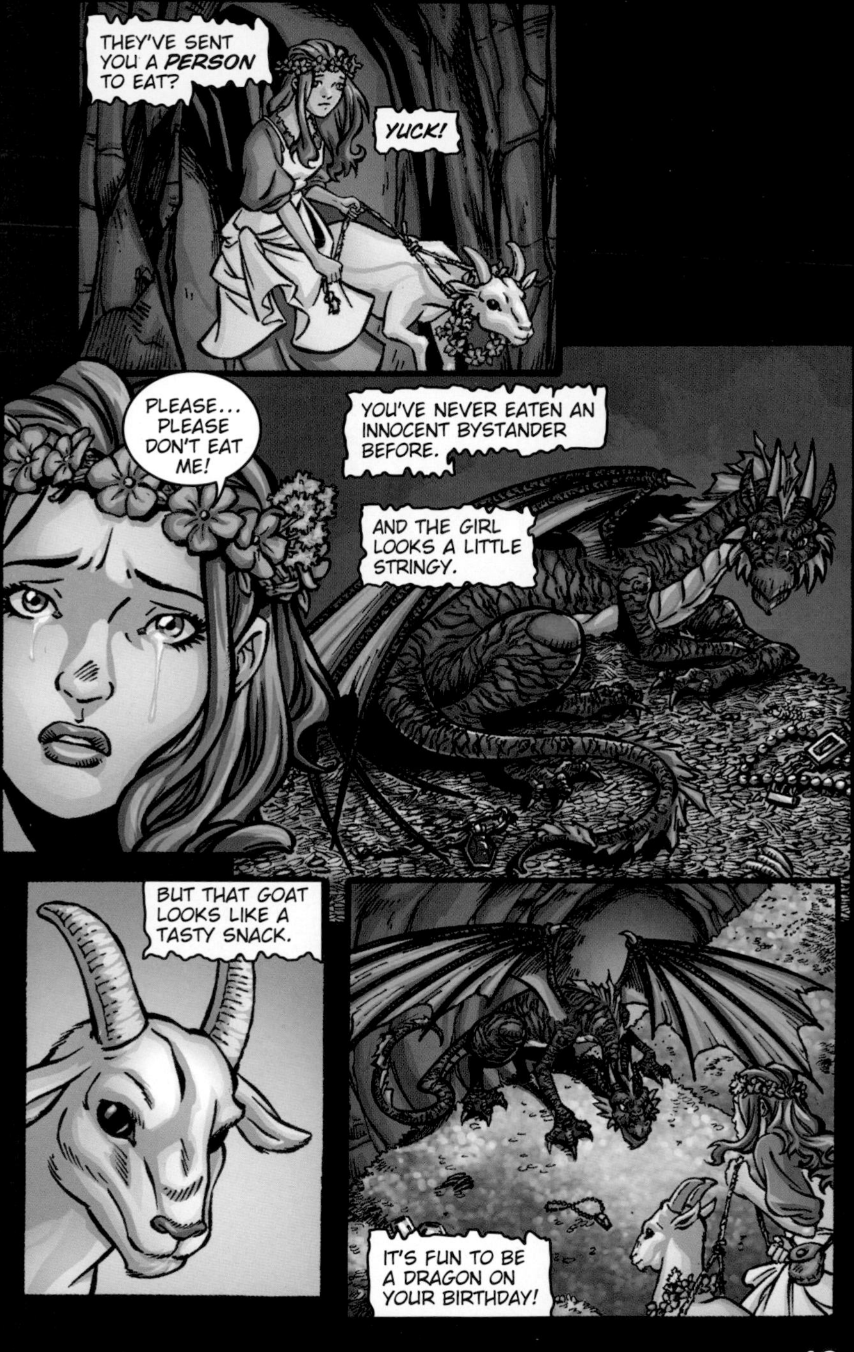
THEY'VE SENT YOU A *PERSON* TO EAT?
YUCK!
PLEASE... PLEASE DON'T EAT ME!
YOU'VE NEVER EATEN AN INNOCENT BYSTANDER BEFORE.
AND THE GIRL LOOKS A LITTLE STRINGY.
BUT THAT GOAT LOOKS LIKE A TASTY SNACK.
IT'S FUN TO BE A DRAGON ON YOUR BIRTHDAY!

GO ON TO THE NEXT PAGE.

Your stomach rumbles.

WILL YOU . . .

. . . quickly gobble up the goat to satisfy your stomach?
TURN TO PAGE 42.

. . . have a little fun with both of them first?
TURN TO PAGE 26.

It's so exciting to breathe real fire for the first time. You swoop in wide circles over the village, blasting every hut and fanning the flames with your powerful wings. When the people run, you chase them with little flares and hissing streams of fire.

Pretty soon, almost nothing is left standing. All the villagers have run to the woods. They won't be coming back—their huts are smoldering piles of burnt straw and ashes. Your fun is all over for now. Maybe even forever. *Oops.*

It looks a little lonely around here now.

Your next birthday won't be quite as exciting without any villagers left to celebrate it.

THE END

You make up your mind. You stop chasing the villagers and turn back toward your mountain. After a quick stop to grab your clock, you're on your way.

You head in the opposite direction from the village and fly toward the sunset. You haven't gone very far in this direction before, so many of the sights are new.

At first you see mostly forest. But after a while, you fly over a stream and then a strange kind of field. It's much larger than the village gardens, with big squares of different colors where different plants are growing. It looks like a giant chessboard.

GO ON TO THE NEXT PAGE.

WHEN YOU GET HUNGRY, YOU SNATCH A GOAT FROM A ROCKY HILLTOP.

WHEN YOU GET THIRSTY, YOU DRINK FROM A STREAM.

AFTER MANY DAYS OF FLYING...

...YOU SEE ANOTHER AMAZING NEW SIGHT.

THIS HUGE WATER MUST BE THE SEA.

THE CAVES IN THESE CLIFFS WOULD MAKE EXCELLENT DRAGON LAIRS.

GO ON TO THE NEXT PAGE.

This big city has many people in it. Perhaps someone there knows about your clock or knows about dragons. It was probably a human who made your clock, but people can be dangerous.

WILL YOU . . .

. . . head to the city?
TURN TO PAGE 82.

. . . search for a dragon in the cliffs?
TURN TO PAGE 8.

After several more minutes, you decide the knight must have given up, at least for now. You leave the pile of swords, shields, and other heavy objects in place, blocking the tunnel. Maybe you should be more careful from now on.

You climb back to the top of your hoard and dig your clock out from its hiding place. Just as you uncover it, it chimes softly. Your birthday is over at last.

Who knows what next year will bring?

TURN TO PAGE 4.

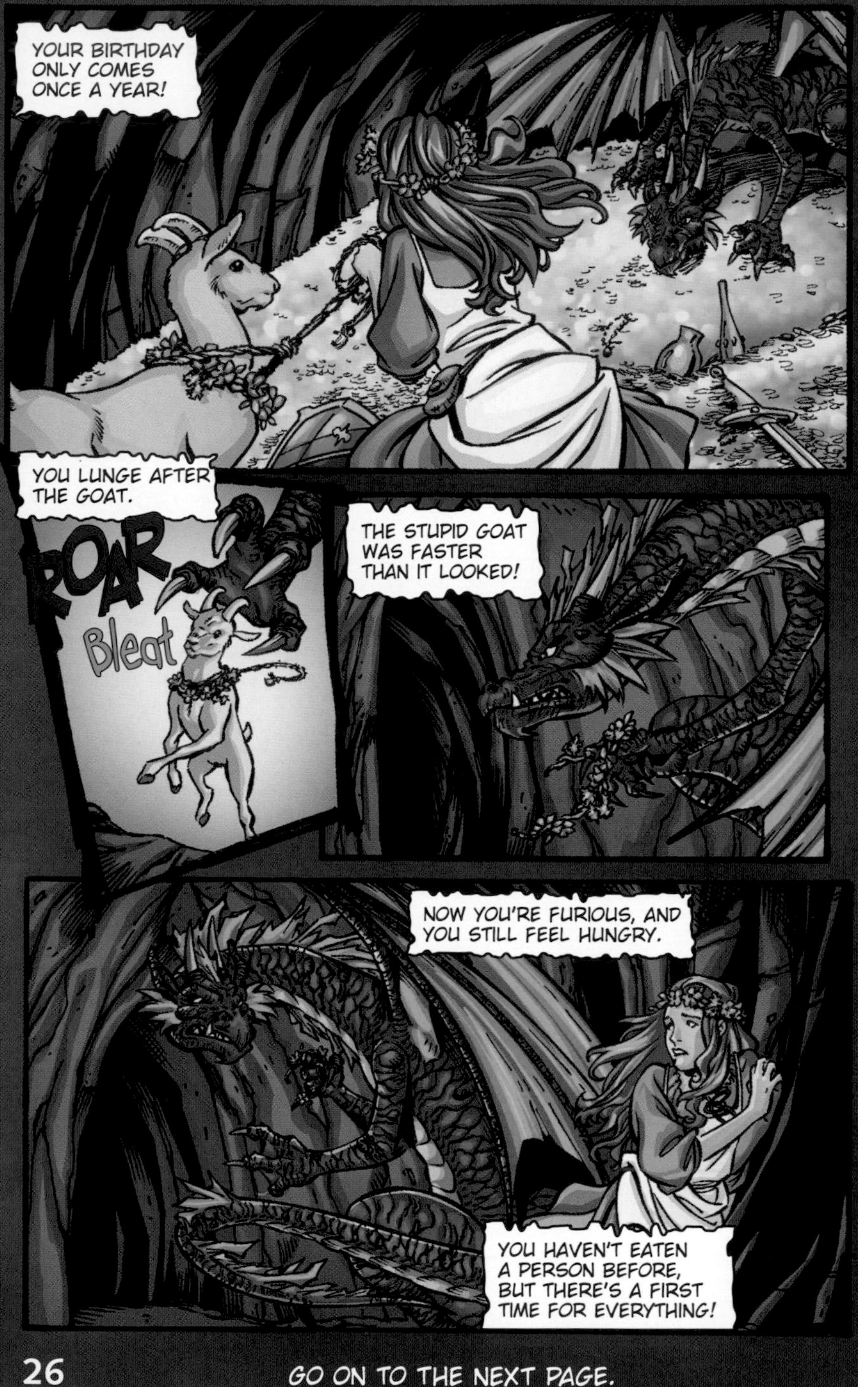
YOUR BIRTHDAY ONLY COMES ONCE A YEAR!
YOU LUNGE AFTER THE GOAT.
ROAR
Bleat
THE STUPID GOAT WAS FASTER THAN IT LOOKED!
NOW YOU'RE FURIOUS, AND YOU STILL FEEL HUNGRY.
YOU HAVEN'T EATEN A PERSON BEFORE, BUT THERE'S A FIRST TIME FOR EVERYTHING!

GO ON TO THE NEXT PAGE.

You're more than ready to try this girl for a snack. But as you step toward her, the girl holds out her hands. "Wait!" she says. "Don't eat me! I can help you!"

You laugh, snorting out smoke. "How can *you* help *me*?" you ask.

"I come from a very old family, one of the first families in the village," the girl says. "My grandmother is a wisewoman, and my brother is a mighty knight."

A knight? That could mean trouble. Knights have been hunting and fighting dragons for hundreds of years. But this girl doesn't really look like she comes from an important family.

"If that is true, how did you end up here?" you ask her.

GO ON TO THE NEXT PAGE.

The girl looks down at her old, tattered dress. "My brother left two years ago on a quest," she says. "My grandmother and I have no one to protect us. Some of the villagers say that my grandmother is a witch."

You're getting a little bored with the silly villagers. "What does any of this have to do with helping me?" you ask.

"My grandmother is a wisewoman who knows a lot of things," she says. "She knows about your timekeeping machine and how to make its magic work. She knows how to make you breathe fire and she knows that something special happens on your one-hundredth birthday!"

Something special? You can hardly believe what she is saying. And you've never thought that your clock could do anything other than keep time.

GO ON TO THE NEXT PAGE.

It would be wonderful if the wisewoman could tell you more about the clock . . . and about how to breathe more than just smoke!

WILL YOU . . .

. . . let the girl go so she can bring back her grandmother?

TURN TO PAGE 51

. . . follow the girl back to her village?

TURN TO PAGE 86.

You charge forward, roaring as loud as you can. The mighty sound of your voice brings small rocks falling down from the sides of the cavern.

The knight moves away until his back is up against the wall. Thin wisps of smoke rise from your nostrils as you claw at his armor. He swings his sword, but it bounces off the hard scales on your shoulder and flies from his hand.

You swipe your front claw with all your might, hitting the knight hard. His armor clanks and crashes as he falls to the ground.

You try to catch your breath as you wait. He doesn't get up again. You see the sword lying on your cave floor, gleaming in the torchlight. It's a nice sword. The grip is wrapped with gold, and it looks like it has real jewels on it.

That will make a *fine* addition to your collection!

THE END

AFTER SOME THOUGHT, YOU PICK ONE CAVE TO EXPLORE.

THE ENTRANCE IS JUST LARGE ENOUGH FOR YOU.

YOU DON'T SEE ANY SIGNS OF LIFE.

BUT THEN...

OOOOOH...

GO ON TO THE NEXT PAGE.

WILL YOU . . .

. . . explore more of the cave?
TURN TO PAGE 98.

. . . play with all the new treasure?
TURN TO PAGE 78.

. . . see if any of the other caves are
full of gold too?
TURN TO PAGE 46.

You fly out of the mountaintop to find out why the girl won't come in. From high in the air, you see just her and her grandmother, as she promised.

You swoop down over them. The girl looks scared, but the old woman is smiling calmly. You decide to circle around for one more pass. As you fly low over the ground, a knight steps out of hiding in the trees. This must be the girl's brother—she *did* trick you!

The knight holds up a shield and sword. You're flying too fast to stop or turn away in time, so you fold your wings to your sides and plunge toward the knight with a terrible roar.

As you crash into him, the knight stabs you with his sword, right under your belly where you have no armor. You fall to the ground with a *thump* that shakes the trees. The knight is crushed by your fall—but you know he'll be called a hero for having slain you.

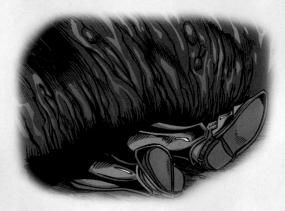

THE END

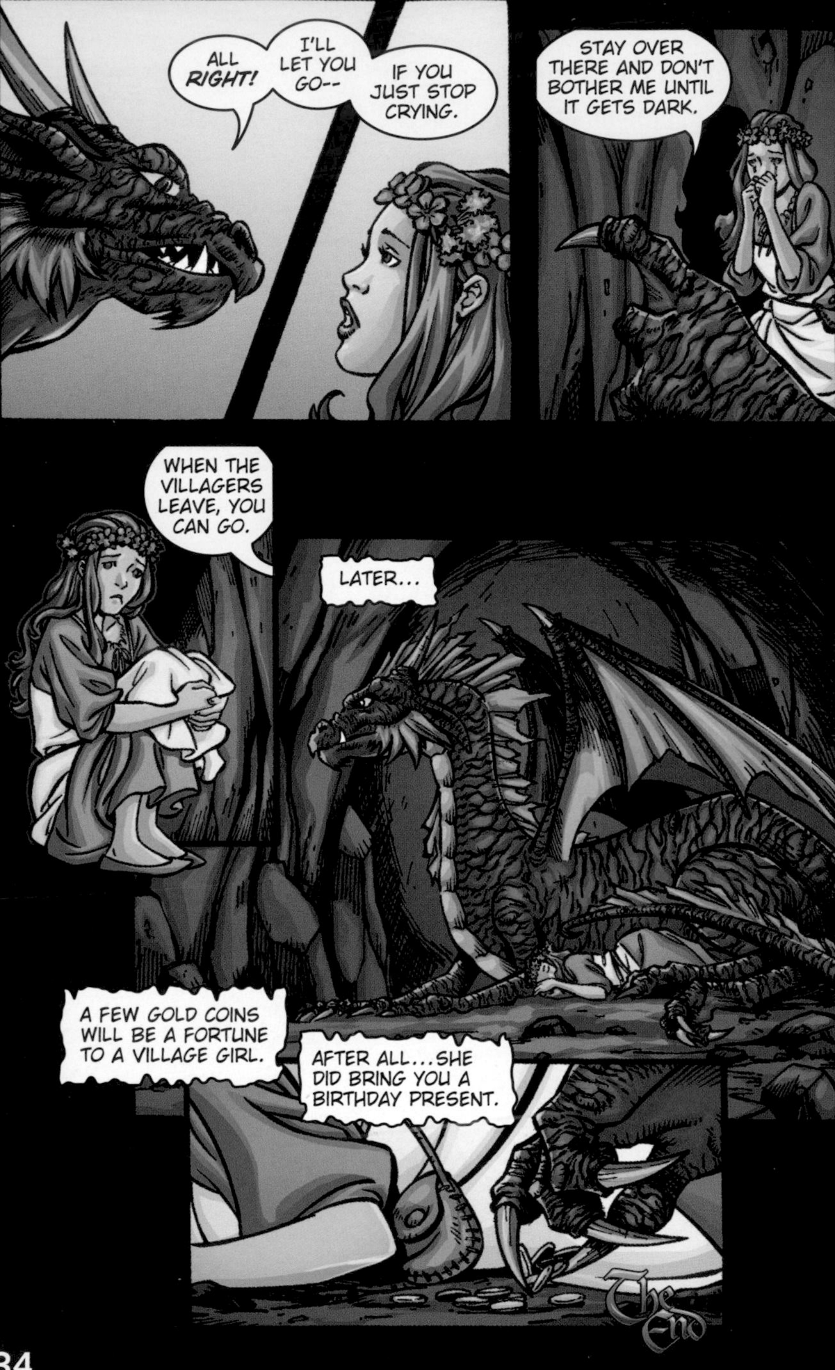

ALL *RIGHT!*
I'LL LET YOU GO--
IF YOU JUST STOP CRYING.
STAY OVER THERE AND DON'T BOTHER ME UNTIL IT GETS DARK.
WHEN THE VILLAGERS LEAVE, YOU CAN GO.
LATER...
A FEW GOLD COINS WILL BE A FORTUNE TO A VILLAGE GIRL.
AFTER ALL...SHE DID BRING YOU A BIRTHDAY PRESENT.
The End

You are surrounded by all sorts of things to experiment with. You set down your clock and move a little lower on the huge heap of treasure. You point your nose toward a deep pile of golden coins and try a small blaze. Nothing happens.

You take a deep breath, open wide, and *ROAR* at the pile of coins. This time the blast comes from deep down inside your chest. By the time you snap your mouth shut, the coins in front of you are all melted together in a shiny lump. You can hardly tell they were coins at all.

GO ON TO THE NEXT PAGE.

THAT WAS IMPRESSIVE!

YOU TRY YOUR FIERY BREATH ON SOMETHING HARDER AND STRONGER THAN GOLD...

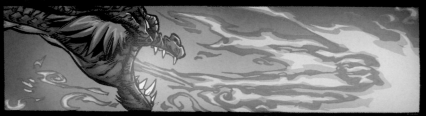

MAYBE YOU CAN REDECORATE!

YESSS!!

HMMM...

GO ON TO THE NEXT PAGE.

This metal shield is so shiny, you can see your reflection in it. You set it on the floor, leaning against the cavern wall, and slither backward a few steps. Just in case.

You aim a mighty bellow of flame at the shield. But the shield doesn't melt. Instead, the fire hits it and bounces right back! Suddenly, you are swallowed up in your own flames. They are hotter than any torch or candle. Your scales are burning!

The shield must have been magic. You wish you had learned more about the things in your hoard . . . and about your own fire . . . but it's too late now. This is . . .

THE END

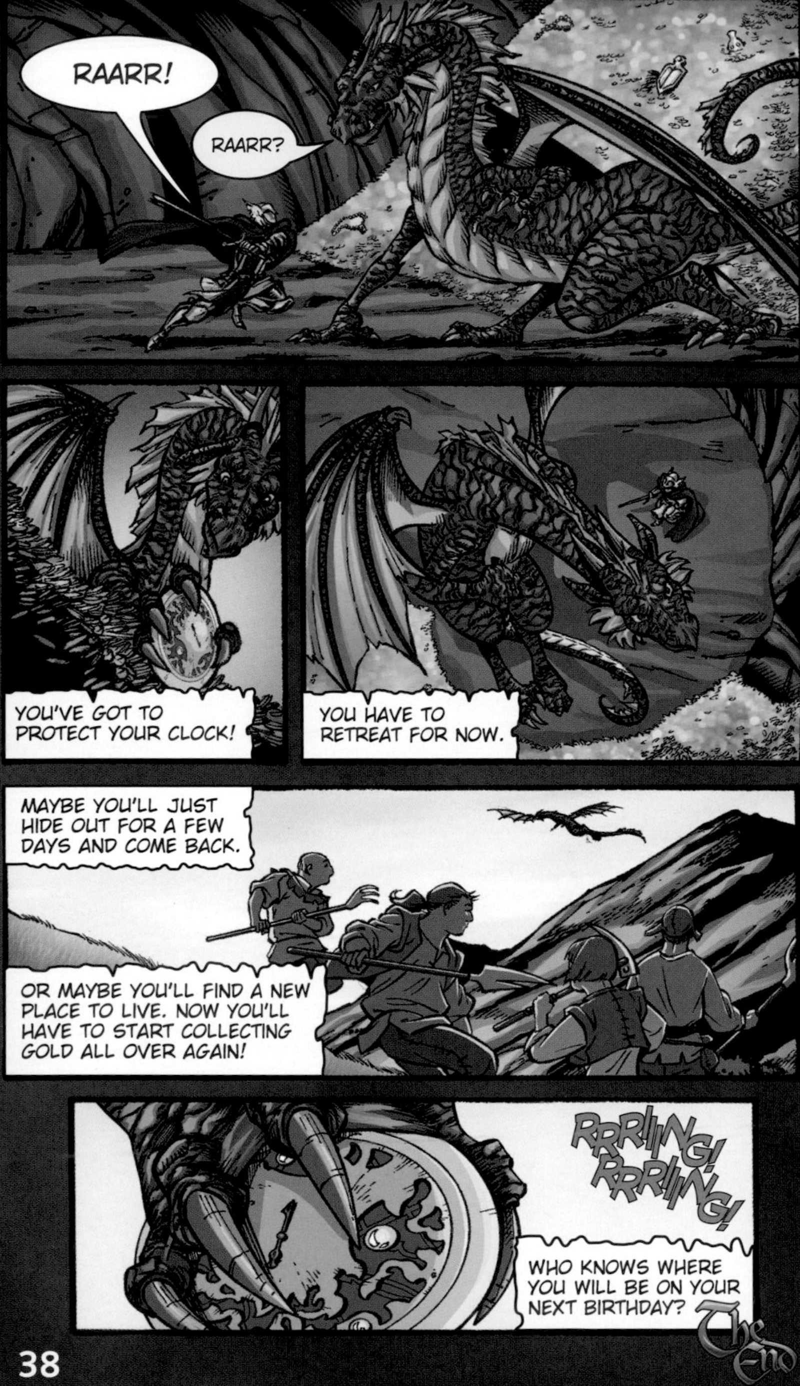
RAARR!
RAARR?
YOU'VE GOT TO PROTECT YOUR CLOCK!
YOU HAVE TO RETREAT FOR NOW.
MAYBE YOU'LL JUST HIDE OUT FOR A FEW DAYS AND COME BACK.
OR MAYBE YOU'LL FIND A NEW PLACE TO LIVE. NOW YOU'LL HAVE TO START COLLECTING GOLD ALL OVER AGAIN!
RRRIIING! RRRIIING!
WHO KNOWS WHERE YOU WILL BE ON YOUR NEXT BIRTHDAY?
The End

You stretch out one magnificent wing toward the girl. "Climb up on my back," you say, "and I'll take you out."

She hesitates until you shake your wing impatiently. Then she scrambles onto your back. You leap upward, beating your mighty wings. You hurtle out of an opening at the very top of the mountain.

A group of villagers is still crowded around the base of the mountain where the tunnel leads into your lair. You can't resist having a little fun with them! You turn sharply in the air and dive down toward them. Just as you swoop over their heads, the girl on your back shouts, *"Now!"* and leaps to the ground.

This was a trap!

You beat the air with your wings, trying to get away. Then you hear the loud *twangs* of bowstrings. You're hit with arrows from every side. The last thing you feel is an arrow piercing your heart.

THE END

You point your snout toward a nearby tree and let out a small roar. A puff of flame shoots out of your mouth and lights up the tree's leaves and branches. Grinning, you take to the air again and follow the villagers.

Even though they are running fast, you catch up with them quickly. The knight is at the back of the group, and he keeps looking over his shoulder. When he sees how close you are, he turns his horse around to face you. He raises his shield to protect his face and points the sharp tip of his sword right at you.

GO ON TO THE NEXT PAGE.

WILL YOU . . .

. . . just fly over the knight and go to the village?
TURN TO PAGE 91.

. . . get rid of him once and for all?
TURN TO PAGE 65.

The girl presses herself against the rocky wall. The villagers are still shouting outside. You're not sure why they decided to send you a human this time around, but they seem determined not to let her escape.

The goat leans against her skirt, bleating sadly. You almost feel sorry for it.

Almost, you think, as you lunge forward . . .

GO ON TO THE NEXT PAGE.

Bleat

YOU WERE RIGHT.

munch crunch crack

THE GOAT DID MAKE A TASTY SNACK.

YOU WEREN'T GOING TO EAT THE SKINNY GIRL, BUT YOU STILL FEEL HUNGRY.

GIVE ME ONE GOOD REASON WHY I SHOULDN'T EAT YOU TOO.

B-B-B-BECAUSE I DIDN'T DO ANYTHING TO YOU.

NEITHER DID THE GOAT.

GO ON TO THE NEXT PAGE.

You want to get the pesky girl out of your lair.
But what if the villagers insist you accept their "gift"?

WILL YOU . . .

. . . chase her out?
TURN TO PAGE 77.

. . . let her climb on your back and take her
out through your secret exit?
TURN TO PAGE 39.

. . . let her hide until the villagers go home and
sneak her out after dark?
TURN TO PAGE 34.

You let out an earth-shattering roar. "Now, why'd you do that?" a voice asks from behind you.

Startled, you nearly fall off the roof. You whirl around and see . . . another dragon sitting just a few feet away. "I-I didn't see you there!" you say.

"I know." The other dragon smiles toothily. "I can make myself almost invisible. I'll teach you how, if you like."

You bring out your clock. "Can you teach me anything about this?"

The dragon laughs. "Of course. All dragons have a special magic item. Mine is a compass." Before you can ask what a magic *compass* is, the other dragon says, "Let's leave before the humans get here."

"Where are we going?"

"To the cliffs by the sea, where all the dragons live." But you saw those cliffs—there weren't any dragons! As if reading your mind, the new dragon says, "There are dragons everywhere. We like to perch on rooftops. But you have to know how to see us."

You follow as the other dragon flies away on silent wings, unnoticed by any of the humans below. You've found what you were searching for. A new friendship has begun, but for your first dragon quest this is . . .

THE END

YOU COULD PLAY WITH THIS GOLD FOR HOURS.

BUT YOU REALLY SHOULD CHECK THE OTHER CAVES BEFORE IT'S TOO DARK.

YOU DON'T HAVE TIME TO DO MORE THAN POKE YOUR HEAD INTO EACH ONE.

THEY ALL SEEM TO BE EMPTY, ANYWAY.

GO ON TO THE NEXT PAGE.

The sunlight is fading as you check one last cave. You're just about to give up. You're tired, and it's getting hard to see very far inside. But when you squint and stare into the darkness of the last cavern, you see footprints. Four big feet with big claws . . . just like you have. Another dragon!

"Hello?" you growl. The tunnel makes your voice echo many times, getting louder and louder. When the echoes finally fade away, you hear something moving inside the cave. Someone comes to the entrance, but it isn't a dragon—it's a *human*. A young man, as a matter of fact. "Hello," he says.

You don't want another fight with humans. You say quietly, "I'm sorry. I was looking for a dragon. I saw these footprints and I thought . . ."

GO ON TO THE NEXT PAGE.

"You were right," says the stranger. "There is a dragon here."

"Where?" you ask.

"Right here," he answers, smiling. "I am a dragon, just like you are. And you can be a human, just like me."

"Wh-what?" you stammer.

"I'll explain everything," he says. "Do you have your clock?"

He knows about the clock? You hesitate only a moment, then say eagerly, "Tell me all about it."

And so he does. "I can show you how to use your clock to change into a human, if you want to," he explains. "But it only works once a year, while it's chiming for your birthday."

You hand your clock to the stranger. He studies it for a moment and says, "Aha—you've just had a birthday. You'll have to wait another year, now."

You are full of questions, and obviously this person has a lot of answers! You give him a dragonish smile. You have a feeling the time will fly between now and your next birthday.

THE END

IT FEELS GOOD TO GIVE IN TO YOUR ANGER AT LAST!

EVEN IF IT MEANS YOU WON'T GET A BIRTHDAY PRESENT NEXT YEAR...

The End

Maybe you'll have a chance to reason with someone indoors. You glide down to the front of the dark building and tap on the door with one claw. To your surprise, the door swings open.

You peer into the darkness. Suddenly a figure jumps out. He's dressed in a wizard's robes and pointed hat, and you freeze in shock. The wizard throws something at you, and you feel a spray of burning waterdrops across your face and chest.

The man shouts words you don't understand. You feel dizzy . . . *changed*. You look at your claws and see that they're tiny now next to the huge blades of grass.

And your clock! It's more than twice your size! The wizard picks it up, and you try to blast him with fire . . . but nothing happens. He looks down at you with a little smile on his wrinkled, wise-looking face. "Here in the city we know how to deal with *your* kind," he says. "Now, go on, little bird. *Shoo*."

Bird? How dare he call you a bird? You skitter through the grass and climb up on a rocky wall. Just then a sparrow flutters down and settles next to you. It's bigger than you are! It peers at you with a bright, beady black eye, then ruffles its feathers with a shrug.

As the sparrow hops away, you realize your life as a dragon has reached . . .

THE END

I WILL FETCH MY GRANDMOTHER BACK HERE. SHE'LL TELL YOU EVERYTHING!

YOU HAD BETTER BE TELLING THE TRUTH.

I THINK THE VILLAGERS HAVE ALL GONE HOME.

THEN GO ON. GET OUT OF HERE BEFORE I CHANGE MY MIND!

BE BACK AT DAWN-- OR I WILL COME AND FIND YOU!

AND... EAT YOU!

The night passes slowly. You can't sleep at all. You keep thinking about what the village girl said. If she's telling the truth, you might be about to learn all kinds of new things about yourself.

You don't remember having parents or even knowing another dragon. Once you thought you saw another dragon in the distance, swooping through the sky just like you do when you want to stretch your wings. But when you tried to get closer, the flying creature disappeared. You aren't even sure now that it really was a dragon.

Finally, your clock shows that it's almost morning. You hear footsteps in the tunnel outside.

"Um . . . Dragon?" the girl's voice calls. "I'm here with my grandmother, but she is afraid to come in. Won't you come outside?"

GO ON TO THE NEXT PAGE.

Why won't the girl come back in?

WILL YOU . . .

. . . demand that she bring in her grandmother?
TURN TO PAGE 93.

. . . tell her to wait outside while you fly out through your personal secret exit?
TURN TO PAGE 33.

You bury your clock under a pile of coins and leap into the air. No one's going to come all the way into your lair if you can help it! But you are too big to leave through the narrow tunnel the villagers use to bring you their birthday gifts.

Instead, you fly up and out of the top of the mountain through your very own secret exit. No villager has ever dared to climb high enough on your mountain to find this way into your cave.

You come out the top and swoop around to look down. You see a large crowd of people below.

GO ON TO THE NEXT PAGE.

YOU FLY VERY FAST TOWARD THE VILLAGERS...

LET'S SEE HOW THEY LIKE THIS...

ROARRR

IN SPITE OF YOUR LOUDEST ROAR, THE VILLAGERS DON'T LOOK VERY SCARED.

UH OH...

...*THIS* IS A FIRST!

GO ON TO THE NEXT PAGE.

This knight looks tall and strong. The villagers have never threatened you before.

WILL YOU . . .

. . . return to the safety of your lair?
TURN TO PAGE 80.

. . . stand your ground, even if it means a fight?
TURN TO PAGE 10.

You are so tempted to try out your flames on the clock, but you're even more afraid of hurting the precious object. You realize that you don't really know much about it, even though you have held it and looked at it so many times.

You know that there is a wisewoman in the village . . . a very old human woman who claims to do some magic. There are knights nearby who have traveled all over the world. Knights are dangerous, but surely they have learned many things from their journeys.

And you'll never forget that once you saw a huge, flying creature in the distance that might have been another dragon.

GO ON TO THE NEXT PAGE.

Maybe you can find someone, human or dragon, who knows about your clock and why you can suddenly breathe fire.

WILL YOU . . .

. . . try to find the village wisewoman?
TURN TO PAGE 96.

. . . fly off in the direction of the dragon you once saw?
TURN TO PAGE 111.

Now's your chance to make sure the villagers treat you right from now on. You stay in the air, circling the village until the knight finally rides in. "What do you want?" he shouts.

Want? Just who attacked first?

"Never threaten me again!" you bellow. "Leave me alone. Except on my birthday. I want a goat once a year . . ."

You realize the villagers already give you a goat on most birthdays. "Make that *two* goats!" you shout. "Two big, fat ones!"

"And if we agree?" yells the knight.

"I won't do this," you roar back. As you fly over one of the little wooden houses, you spit just the slightest burst of flame. The thatched roof instantly catches fire.

"All right!" the knight shouts. "We agree."

You snatch a goat from its corral as you leave. All this fire-breathing has made you hungry. But it's been a great birthday. And that knight won't get to slay any dragons today.

THE END

Of course you have examined your clock before—very carefully. Over the years, you've looked closely at every inch of it and tried shaking it and picking at it with your claws. Nothing ever seemed to hurt it. The hands just keep moving around the clockface. You don't even have to wind it. The bells chime to tell the hours, and they ring a different tune every year on your birthday.

Now you try it all again. You hold the clock up close to your face and stare at it until your vision starts to get blurry. You blink and stare at it some more. It looks the same as always. Beautiful and covered with jewels. Your most precious possession.

GO ON TO THE NEXT PAGE.

YOU SEE NOTHING DIFFERENT...

...TRY AS YOU MIGHT.

NOTHING!

YOU TAKE A DEEP BREATH...

WAIT!

WHAT IF YOUR LITTLE TEST BURNS IT UP OR BREAKS IT?

GO ON TO THE NEXT PAGE.

You really want to know what effect your fire breath might have on your special clock.

WILL YOU . . .

. . . go ahead and blast it?
TURN TO PAGE 15.

. . . seek out more information first?
TURN TO PAGE 57.

You turn away from the ships. Several arrows bounce off the scales on your back, and more arrows swoosh past your tail as you head toward the city.

There are many large houses overlooking the harbor. These houses are much larger than anything you have seen, except for a castle. As the sun sinks lower in the sky, lights appear in many windows. You fly low along the cliff's edge, trying to look into the houses.

You spot a familiar-looking building. It reminds you of the village meeting hall, only much, much larger. You fly toward it and perch on its high roof.

You must find a way to talk to someone
without being attacked.

WILL YOU . . .

. . . bellow for attention?
TURN TO PAGE 45.

. . . creep down and look inside the big hall?
TURN TO PAGE 50.

You open wide and roar directly at the pesky knight. A huge blast of flame pours out of your mouth. But his shield protects him. The fire bounces off it! The knight spurs his horse toward you, and you try again . . . *Rrrraaarrrr!* A hotter blast of fire!

The knight skillfully shields himself and his horse. He charges toward you, swinging his sword. You lower your head and raise your claws. Just as you strike, the knight pulls on the reins and turns his horse sideways, and you just miss him.

The knight's sharp sword cuts a long slice in your belly as his horse gallops past. You sink slowly to the ground. You try to fight back with one last fireball. But all that comes from your mouth is a wisp of smoke.

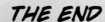

THE END

"Very well," you say with great dignity. "I will spare your family . . . for now. But you have to tell me everything you know!"

"I will keep my word," the old woman says. "But first, I must tell the villagers they are safe."

You pull your head out of the doorway and see that some of the villagers have crept out of their huts. A few brave ones are forming a circle around you. Some of them are carrying weapons—pitchforks, hoes, and other farming tools. The villagers could hurt you if they work together. You sit up on your haunches and raise your wings high. Even the bravest villagers stop in their tracks.

The old woman hobbles out of her hut. "Stand down, stand down," she tells them. "This dragon comes seeking knowledge."

"Yes, knowledge," you agree.

GO ON TO THE NEXT PAGE.

DO NOT BE AFRAID!

MAY WE RIDE ON YOUR BACK? THE PLACE WE MUST GO IS FAR AWAY.

WELL... I SUPPOSE SO...

WHERE ARE WE GOING?

TO THE RUINS ON THE HILLTOP, ON THE OTHER SIDE OF YOUR MOUNTAIN.

YOU'VE SEEN THE RUINS FROM A LONG DISTANCE...

...BUT YOU'VE NEVER GIVEN THEM MUCH THOUGHT.

THE OLD WOMAN SEEMS TO KNOW SOMETHING ABOUT THE MYSTERIOUS PLACE.

The two women take so long poking around in the ruins that you start to feel hungry again.

WILL YOU . . .

. . . satisfy your hunger and return to your lair to sleep off your large meal?
TURN TO PAGE 85.

. . . eat the girl to scare her grandmother into talking?
TURN TO PAGE 90.

. . . pretend you're leaving and see what they do?
TURN TO PAGE 110.

. . . try to scare them both to get some information?
TURN TO PAGE 101.

Maybe you should try one more time to show you don't mean any harm. The arrows don't hurt much. You can dodge them or burn them into ashes as they fly toward you. You glide in close to a small ship. It has fewer men than the others and not as many tall poles—masts—with ropes hanging from them.

A handful of men are gathered around a large, black object. You can't see what it is. As you swoop down even lower, they scatter. Now you can see they have a cannon, and its fuse is already lit. You twist in the air, trying to get away, but you hear a loud *BOOM* as the cannon fires. Your fire goes out as you fall with a crash into the sea.

THE END

You lower yourself slowly to the ground, keeping your head down. Several of the people approaching you are carrying large muskets, but bullets don't hurt you. You try to look as harmless as possible.

You see that one of the humans is just a child . . . younger than the village girl you almost had for breakfast a few days ago. Your wings droop slightly.

A tall man says to the girl, "Go on, Sally. He won't hurt you." The little girl smiles and walks right up to you. You're too surprised to do anything but sit still. She's holding a beautiful, ornate golden necklace with sparkling green jewels.

"This belonged to our dragon, Blaze," she says. "He was very old, and he died nine days ago. Won't you stay with us? Be our new dragon, and help keep us safe?"

You do the math quickly. Poor old Blaze died on your birthday. Somehow you felt that happen, inside. This must be what you have been searching for.

"Yes!" you say happily, and a tiny flame flicks out between your teeth. The people laugh. They seem happy too.

Who needs a golden hoard when you have a new family?

THE END

SNIFF...

SNUFFLE...

YOU GET A STRONG WHIFF OF THE GIRL'S SCENT AND HER GRANDMOTHER'S TOO. YOU CAN TRACK THEM BOTH.

YOU *WILL* FIND THE GIRL.

GO ON TO THE NEXT PAGE.

You've found them! You sneak around the side of the hut and push your head through the doorway. The wooden beams splinter on either side. The girl screams, but the old woman hardly moves at all. "Hush, child," she says calmly. "Take the candle and set it on the table, before we set the hut on fire."

The girl obeys, but she keeps an eye on you the whole time. The old woman gets to her feet slowly. She is tiny—even smaller than her granddaughter—and very wrinkled. You see a wooden staff, probably to help her walk, leaning against the wall nearby.

"Well, it seems you have found us," the old woman says to you. "I suppose you are going to eat us. But if, instead, you promise never to hurt my family, I will tell you all the secrets I know about you and your treasure."

GO ON TO THE NEXT PAGE.

She and her granddaughter have
already tricked you once.

WILL YOU . . .

. . . eat them both and go home?
TURN TO PAGE 16.

. . . agree to listen to the old woman?
TURN TO PAGE 66.

You stick your snout into what seems like at least a hundred cave openings. But all you find are rocks and birds and small animals. If dragons ever did live here, they aren't here now!

When you get too tired to fly anymore, you perch on the cliff's edge and stare out over the ocean. It's too dark now to search, anyway. You can see lights twinkling in the large town you flew over before.

You turn and look away from the sea. In the distance, you see more lights twinkling, faint and very far away. It must be another big town!

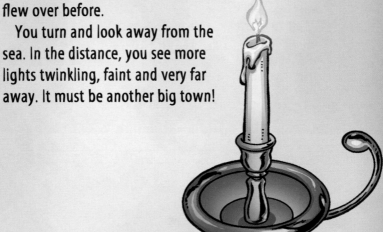

GO ON TO THE NEXT PAGE.

AS TIRED AS YOU ARE, YOU STRUGGLE BACK INTO THE AIR.

YOU REALIZE YOUR QUEST MUST GO ON.

YOU FLY SLOWLY ALL NIGHT...

...STOPPING ONLY WHEN YOU HAVE TO REST.

FINALLY, MORNING COMES.

YOU CAN SEE THE CITY...

IT'S AMAZING-- AND A LITTLE SCARY.

YOU SPOT SOME OPEN FIELDS AND DECIDE TO LAND THERE.

YOU MAY EVEN FIND A SHEEP FOR BREAKFAST.

UH OH. WHAT'S THIS?

WILL YOU . . .

. . . act as meek and friendly as you can?
TURN TO PAGE 70.

. . . warn them to stay back?
TURN TO PAGE 103.

A little smoke drifts from your nostrils as you say, "Go on. Get out!"

The girl turns and runs. Will the villagers let her escape? It doesn't sound like it. Your sharp ears pick up everything. The villagers sound scared. They yell at her to go back.

The girl stumbles back into your lair with two men holding her arms. Behind them are more villagers. One of them is carrying a pitchfork, one has a hoe, and two have torches.

"Please," says one of the men. "Do not be angry with us!"

"Take this special present for your one-hundredth birthday!" says another.

It's nice of them to remember this is an important day. And you *are* still hungry. You gobble up the girl. Then you gobble up the rest of the villagers too. When you're done, you feel so full, you just might burst! You climb very slowly up to the top of your hoard to curl up around the clock and take a nap.

Maybe next year, the villagers—if there are any left—will know better than to bother you!

THE END

You stand at the bottom of the huge pile of gold. So much treasure . . . so little time!

In fact, you lose track of time as you touch and study everything you can reach. Coins, necklaces, pearls, and sparkly jewels pour through your talons. They clatter and tinkle as they tumble down the pile and scatter across the cave floor.

Clank.

That was definitely a noise *you* didn't make.

Something's behind you!

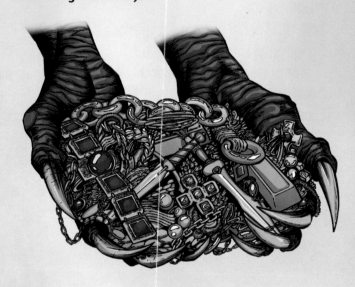

GO ON TO THE NEXT PAGE.

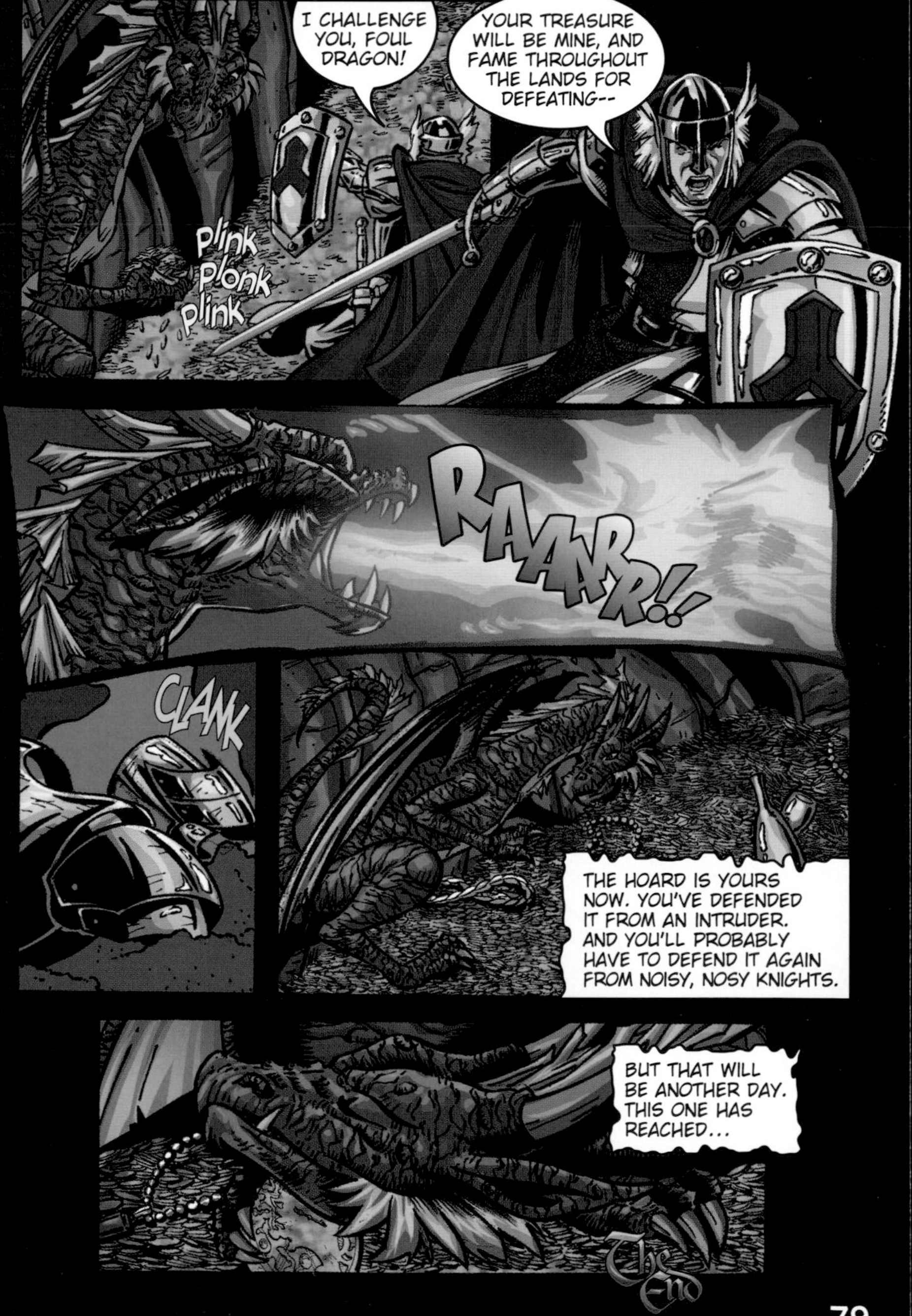
I CHALLENGE YOU, FOUL DRAGON!
YOUR TREASURE WILL BE MINE, AND FAME THROUGHOUT THE LANDS FOR DEFEATING--
Plink Plonk Plink
RAAARR!!
CLANK
THE HOARD IS YOURS NOW. YOU'VE DEFENDED IT FROM AN INTRUDER. AND YOU'LL PROBABLY HAVE TO DEFEND IT AGAIN FROM NOISY, NOSY KNIGHTS.
BUT THAT WILL BE ANOTHER DAY. THIS ONE HAS REACHED...
The End

You haven't fought a knight since you came to live near this village. The people have always seemed afraid of you. They bring you a birthday gift every year and leave you alone the rest of the time.

Now the villagers don't look scared. Beating the air with your wings, you leap upward and fly high over the crowd. As a final good-bye, you give them a loud *ROAR!*

You get back to your cave and land on your pile of treasure with a clinking and tinkling of coins. You hear another noise: loud clanking sounds. Once again, someone is coming through the tunnel!

GO ON TO THE NEXT PAGE.

It could be the knight himself.

WILL YOU . . .

. . . hide in the shadows and try to surprise him?
TURN TO PAGE 107.

. . . try to stop him before he gets inside your lair?
TURN TO PAGE 13.

It's getting late. Soon the sun will start to go down. If you're going to let the city people see you, it's time to take courage and do it!

You glide from the cliff out over the glittering ocean. You fly back up the coast to where many boats are anchored. You've never seen huge boats like these before, with many long oars sticking out from holes on either side. As you come closer, men on the boats spot you. They start pointing. You hear shouts.

GO ON TO THE NEXT PAGE.

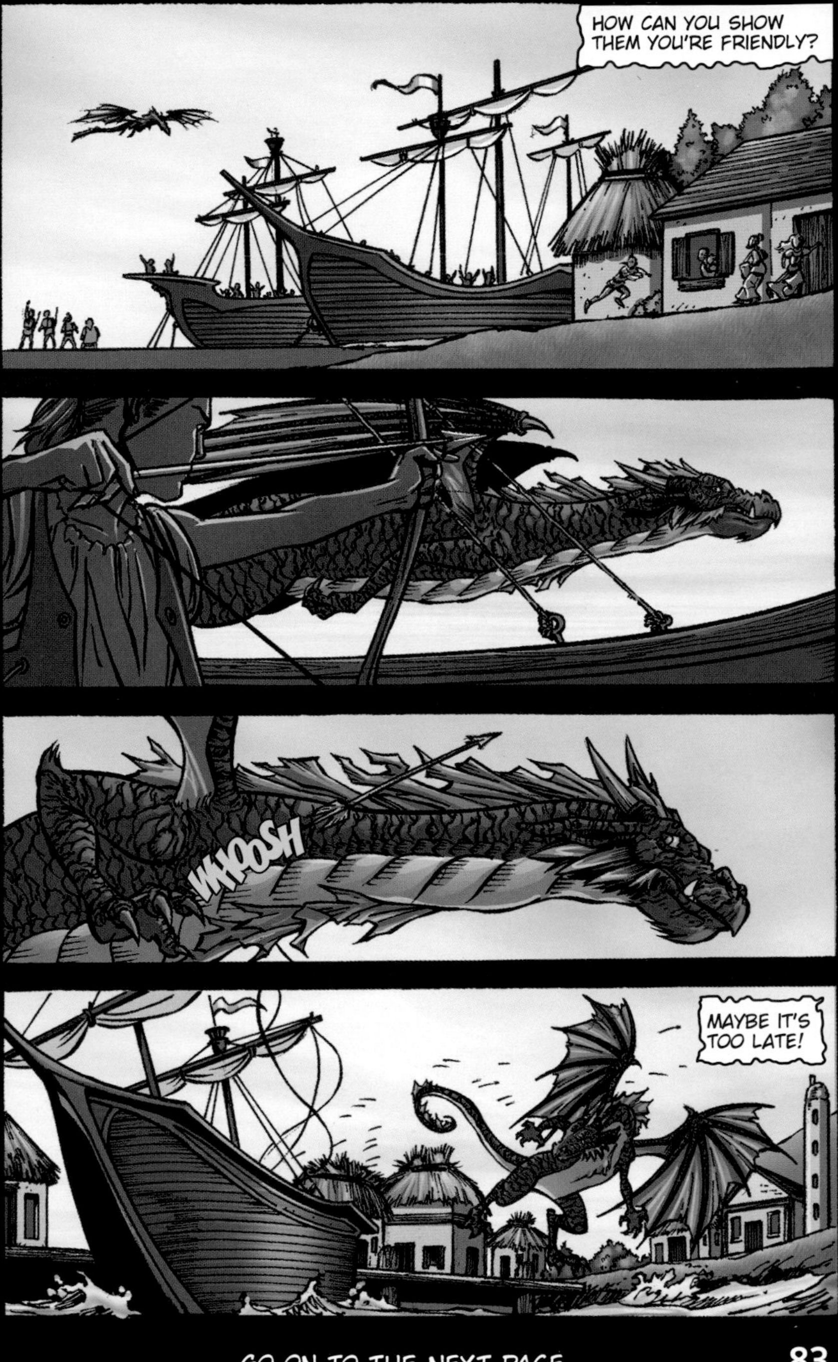
HOW CAN YOU SHOW THEM YOU'RE FRIENDLY?
WHOOSH
MAYBE IT'S TOO LATE!

GO ON TO THE NEXT PAGE.

These men on the ships are just as dangerous as the villagers near home.

WILL YOU . . .

. . . see whether the people in the city are nicer?
TURN TO PAGE 63.

. . . try one more time to be friendly?
TURN TO PAGE 69.

. . . make them back down by giving them a taste of your new fire?
TURN TO PAGE 109.

Hungry and tired of waiting, you gobble up the girl and her grandmother in just a few bites. The old woman is stringy, but her granddaughter is plump and tasty. When you're finished, you're so full, you decide to take a nap right where you are. After that good meal, you sleep very deeply.

In the night, the villagers come looking for their wisewoman. They carry their torches and their pitchforks, and they know this part of the forest even better than you do.

You never even have a chance to wake up.

THE END

Your curiosity gets the better of you. "All right," you growl, letting a little smoke drift from your nostrils. "I will give you *one* chance to prove your grandmother is a wisewoman." You've always wanted to know more about yourself and your hoard. And now you really want to know what will happen on your hundredth birthday.

But you don't want to risk going to the village in daylight. You point with one claw to the far side of your cave—as far as possible from your own bed on your piles of gold.

"Sit over there," you order the girl. She hurries to obey. "After night falls, we will go to the village and see your grandmother . . . together."

GO ON TO THE NEXT PAGE.

AFTER DARK, YOU TELL THE GIRL TO CLIMB ON YOUR BACK.

YOU'LL GET TO THE VILLAGE MUCH FASTER FLYING THAN SHE WOULD ON FOOT.

PLEASE... GO BACK INTO THE TREES AND WAIT WHILE I TALK TO GRANDMOTHER.

YOU WAIT...

...AND WAIT...

GO ON TO THE NEXT PAGE.

. . . and wait.

You wait long enough to realize something is wrong. Finally, you slide out of the trees and stick your head into the little hut. Even in the dark, you can tell that it's empty. The girl must have snuck out a window.

She tricked you! And she's going to pay for it . . . as soon as you find her.

Or maybe you should punish the whole *village*. You saw a flock of plump sheep in a paddock when you flew over the village. Eating their flocks would make the villagers angry at you instead of just scared. But it sure would feel good.

GO ON TO THE NEXT PAGE.

WILL YOU . . .

. . . teach the humans a lesson
and eat all the sheep?
TURN TO PAGE 49.

. . . find the girl and use your wits to get
some information from her?
TURN TO PAGE 71.

The old woman is still digging in the stones and has her back to you. You grab the girl and pull her toward you as she screams. The old woman turns around quickly. "No!" she cries out. But it's too late. The girl only takes a few bites.

The wisewoman's eyes fill with tears. She opens her fingers to show you what she found in the rocks: a small gold key. "I brought you here to find this," she says. "I was going to tell you how to use it to become the greatest dragon that ever lived. But I won't tell you, now."

You move as quickly as a striking snake, snatching the old woman in your claws. You leap off the hilltop and fly toward the mountain . . . and home.

She seems like a stubborn old woman. But maybe, in time, you'll get her to tell you her secret.

THE END

THE KNIGHT LOOKS READY FOR A LONG, HARD FIGHT.

FORGET THAT!

HERE IT COMES! THE DRAGON!!

RUN!

AIEEEE!

NOOO!!

GO ON TO THE NEXT PAGE.

The villagers run for cover as you come flying overhead. Your mighty wings make a strong wind that tears the roofs off their huts.

WILL YOU . . .

. . . destroy the village?
TURN TO PAGE 21.

. . . just teach them a lesson?
TURN TO PAGE 59.

"NO!" you roar. "Both of you, come inside . . . NOW!"

After a moment, the girl comes in with an old woman all bent over with age. The grandmother's braids are gray under her white cap. But her eyes are dark and piercing.

"Bring me the clock," she says. Her voice is so strong that you hurry to do what she says. You reach out to hand the clock to the old woman. As her fingers touch the clock, she whispers, *"The time is now."*

You hear a sound like thunder. A bright flash of lightning fills the cave. Suddenly you are much, much smaller. You are standing on two bare human feet, looking at your sister and your grandmother. You realize you have been under a spell. You had forgotten you even had a human family!

"How—how long has it been?" you ask your grandmother.

"One hundred days since the dragons captured you," she says. "We had to wait for a way to get close to you. You thought you really were a dragon!"

You look at the huge hoard of treasure. The three of you will live happily ever after!

THE END

You're tempted to chase the fleeing villagers and use your new ability. You've always wanted to breathe fire! Somehow, you've always known you were supposed to. But you could only make little puffs of smoke before today.

Maybe you should go back to your lair instead and test your new talent. As the people run away, you turn in midair and fly home to the mountain and your pile of treasure.

You dig up your clock first to make sure it's safe. Could it have anything to do with the change in you? You have studied it so many times . . . it doesn't look different now. But you are different. You have *fire!*

Some of the things in your hoard might melt if you breathe on them. Some might burn or even blow up. You have coins and chests and things made out of strange, mysterious materials. It could be fun to experiment.

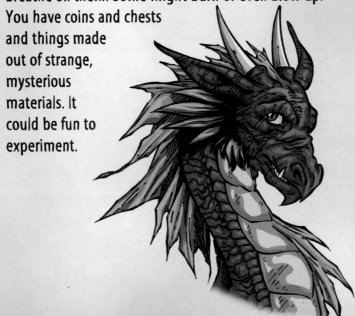

94

GO ON TO THE NEXT PAGE.

WILL YOU . . .

. . . try breathing fire on things in your hoard to see if you can melt them?
TURN TO PAGE 35.

. . . experiment with your clock?
TURN TO PAGE 60.

You tuck your clock under one wing and leap into the air. Leaving the mountain, you fly swiftly toward the village. The people run and hide when they see you, except for the knight. Still mounted on his horse, he stands his ground in front of one of the huts as you swoop in for a landing.

The knight raises his sword. You hold up your foreleg. "Wait," you say. "I only want to see the old grandmother. The wisewoman."

The knight looks surprised and a little suspicious. But he gets off his horse and loops the reins over a nearby post. "Wait here," he says. He goes inside the hut.

GO ON TO THE NEXT PAGE.

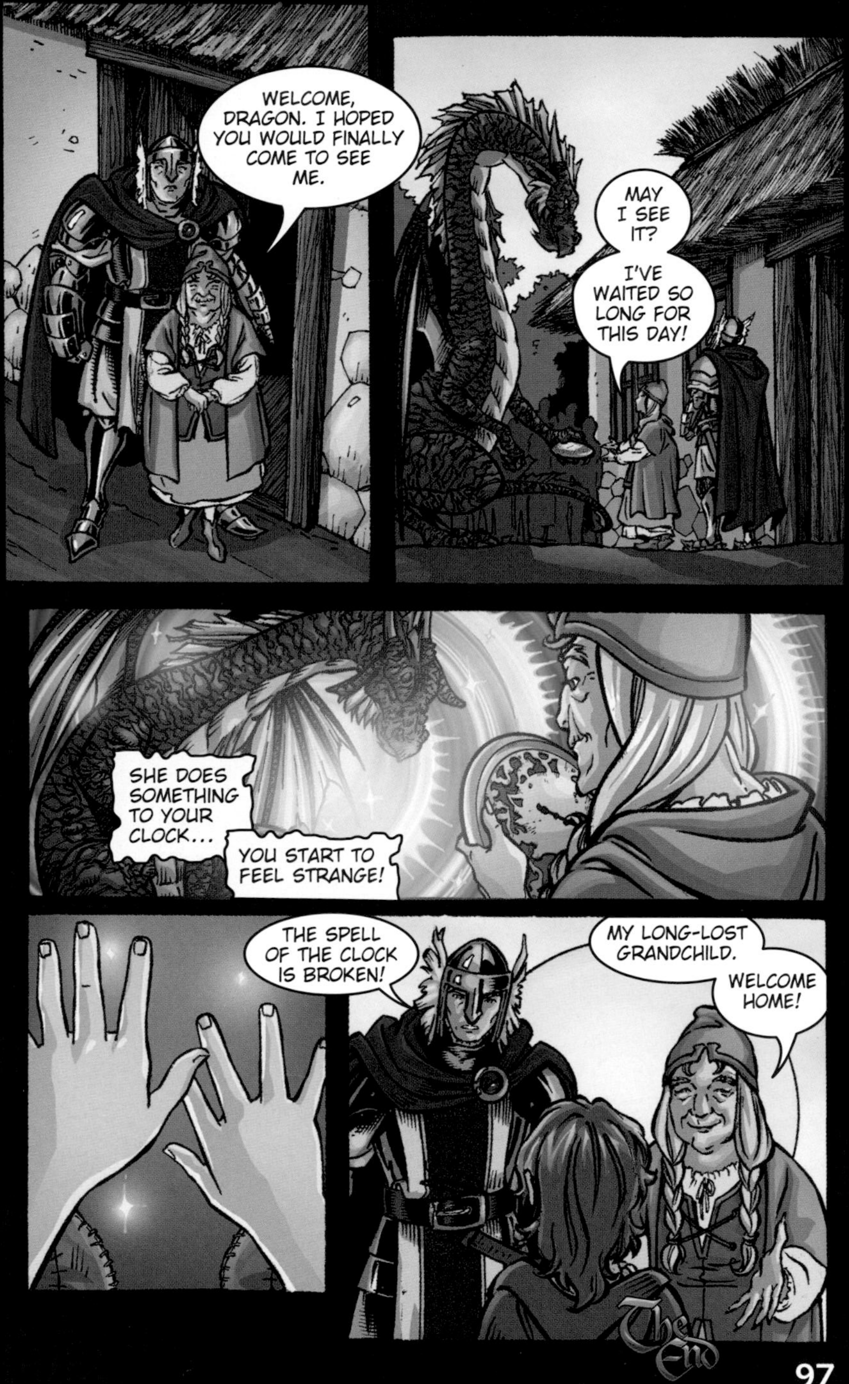
WELCOME, DRAGON. I HOPED YOU WOULD FINALLY COME TO SEE ME.
MAY I SEE IT?
I'VE WAITED SO LONG FOR THIS DAY!
SHE DOES SOMETHING TO YOUR CLOCK...
YOU START TO FEEL STRANGE!
THE SPELL OF THE CLOCK IS BROKEN!
MY LONG-LOST GRANDCHILD.
WELCOME HOME!
The End

AS TEMPTING AS
THE TREASURE IS...

...YOU SHOULD
CHECK OUT
THE REST OF
THIS CAVE.

IT GETS DARKER
AS YOU GO
DEEPER INSIDE.

YOU DECIDE IT MUST
BE EMPTY, UNTIL...

98   GO ON TO THE NEXT PAGE.

You hear the low, threatening growl of a dragon. And since it's not coming from you, it has to be coming from another dragon . . . a *new* dragon. With nowhere to run, you will just have to face it.

You wait where you are as the growling sounds come closer. You can hear footsteps and a tail dragging over the rocks. When the other dragon seems very close, you let out a loud roar just to let it know you're here.

At first you get no answer. Then you hear, "Who's there?"

You clear your long throat, and wisps of smoke drift from your nostrils. "Um, it's me," you answer.

"Who's 'me,' and what are you doing in my cave?" growls the voice.

GO ON TO THE NEXT PAGE.

"I didn't know anyone lived here," you answer.

"Well, *I* do," says the voice.

Finally, the other dragon appears from the dark tunnel. This dragon is smaller than you, but the cave is crowded with both of you squeezed inside. "That's all right," the other dragon says. "I get lonely sometimes with no one but seagulls for company."

"What about the people?" you ask.

"I leave them alone," the other dragon answers. "Where do you come from? Why are you here?"

"It was my birthday . . ." you begin.

"Your *birthday*?" The other dragon squeals in delight and leads you back to the hoard. "Pick out a gift. I *insist!*"

"I can't take any of your things," you say. "Besides, I'm already carrying . . . something."

You think about your own hoard, left unguarded. What if another dragon is snooping around it right now? "I should go," you say.

"I hope you'll come back one day," the other dragon says hopefully. Maybe this dragon, too, has been looking for a friend.

"I will," you promise. And you mean it. You say good-bye for now. It's time for this quest to come to . . .

THE END

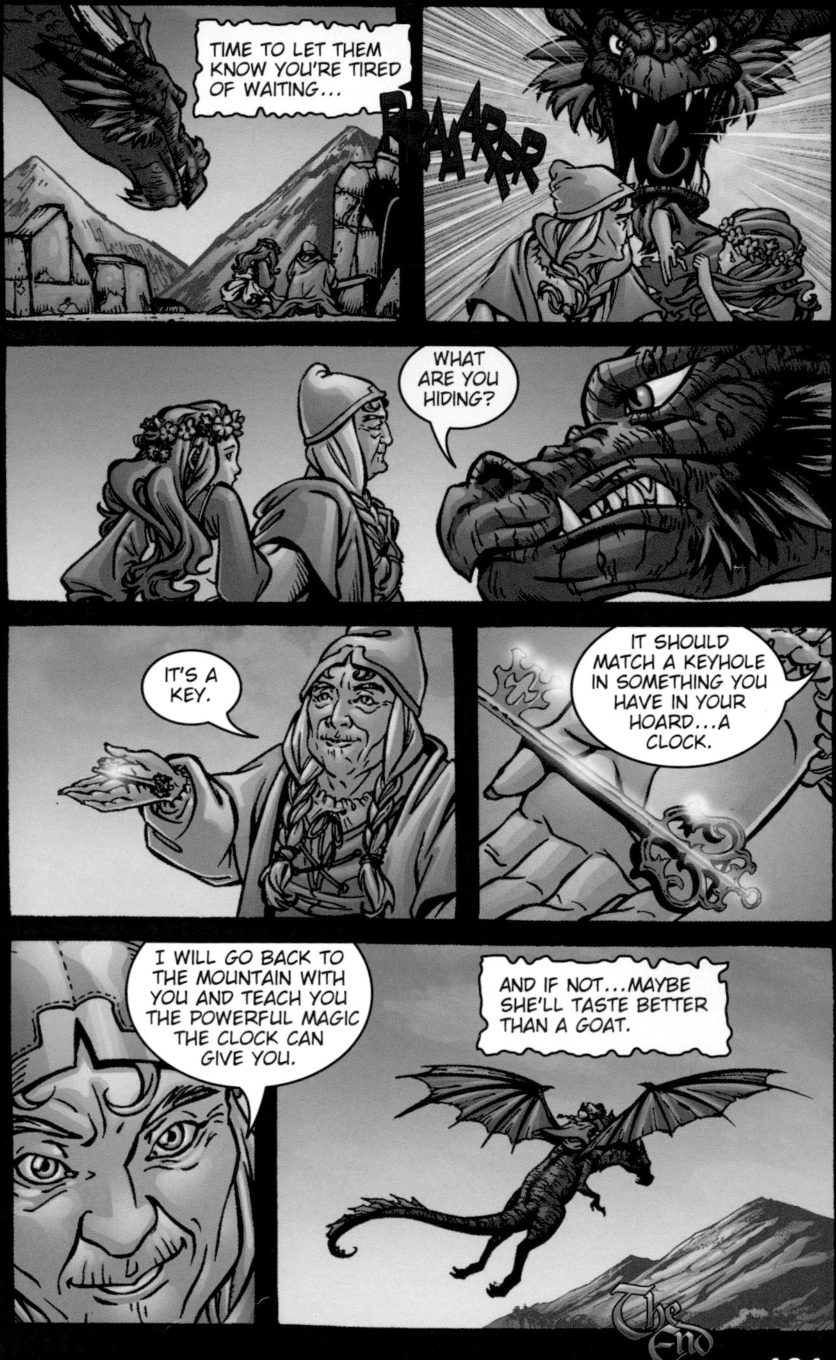
TIME TO LET THEM KNOW YOU'RE TIRED OF WAITING...
RRAAARRR
WHAT ARE YOU HIDING?
IT'S A KEY.
IT SHOULD MATCH A KEYHOLE IN SOMETHING YOU HAVE IN YOUR HOARD...A CLOCK.
I WILL GO BACK TO THE MOUNTAIN WITH YOU AND TEACH YOU THE POWERFUL MAGIC THE CLOCK CAN GIVE YOU.
AND IF NOT...MAYBE SHE'LL TASTE BETTER THAN A GOAT.
The End

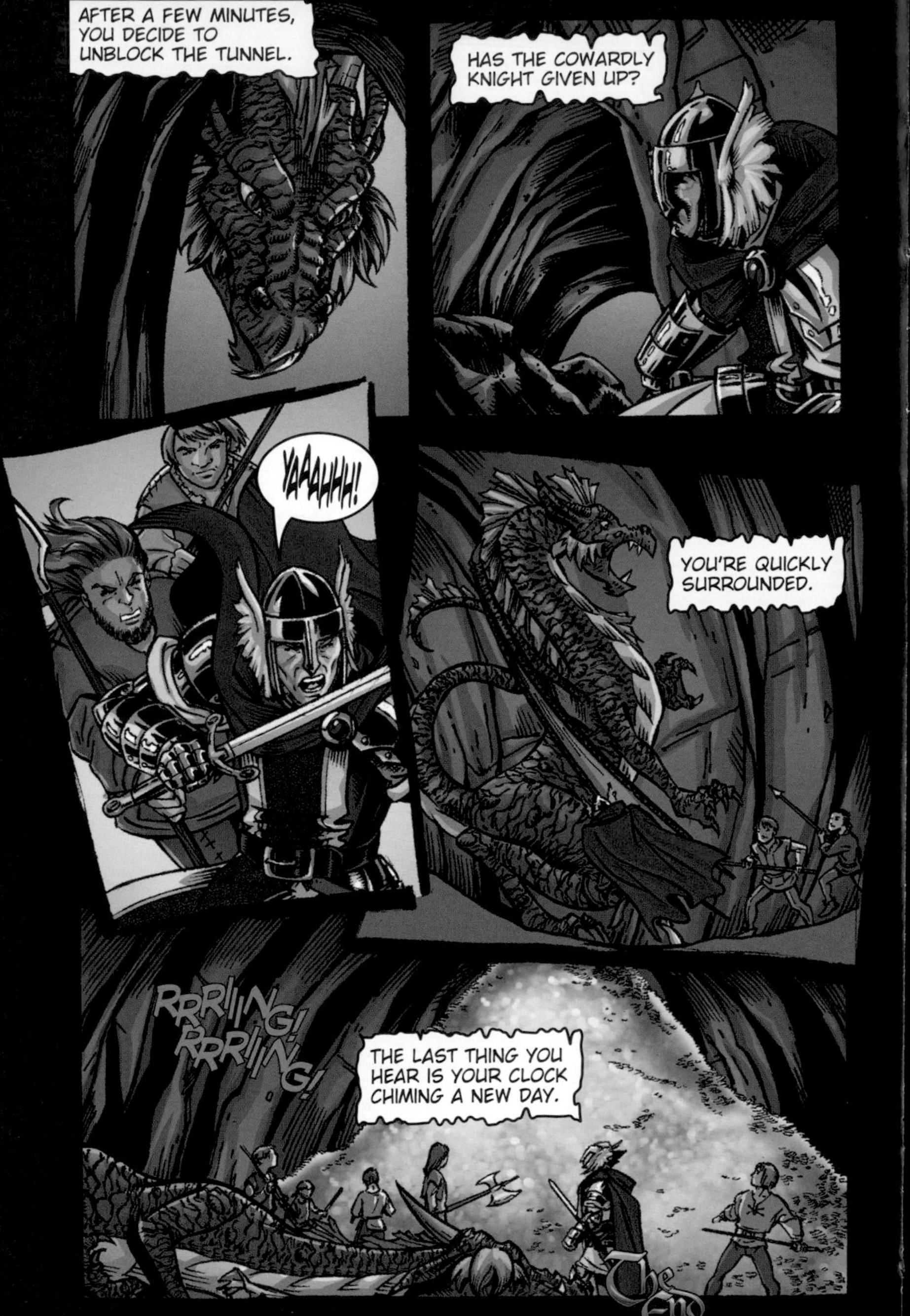
AFTER A FEW MINUTES, YOU DECIDE TO UNBLOCK THE TUNNEL.
HAS THE COWARDLY KNIGHT GIVEN UP?
YAAAHHH!
YOU'RE QUICKLY SURROUNDED.
RRRIIING! RRRIIING!
THE LAST THING YOU HEAR IS YOUR CLOCK CHIMING A NEW DAY.
The End

Humans haven't been so nice to you lately. Raising your wings high, you flex your huge front claws. The people stop short as you roar out a warning.

But after only a moment's pause, two of them raise their muskets and take aim right at you. You rear up just as both guns go off with a loud double explosion. Instead of bullets, the muskets shoot out huge nets that drop right over you. These nets are strong, and your wings are soon tangled. You hear two more shots as you fall to the ground, thrashing.

You struggle for a long time, until you're exhausted and have to lie still. The men bring a team of horses and harness them to the nets holding you.

"This one is strong," one of the men says. "Another good worker for the mines." It's the last thing you hear them say as they drag you away.

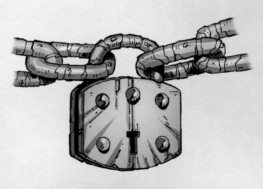

THE END

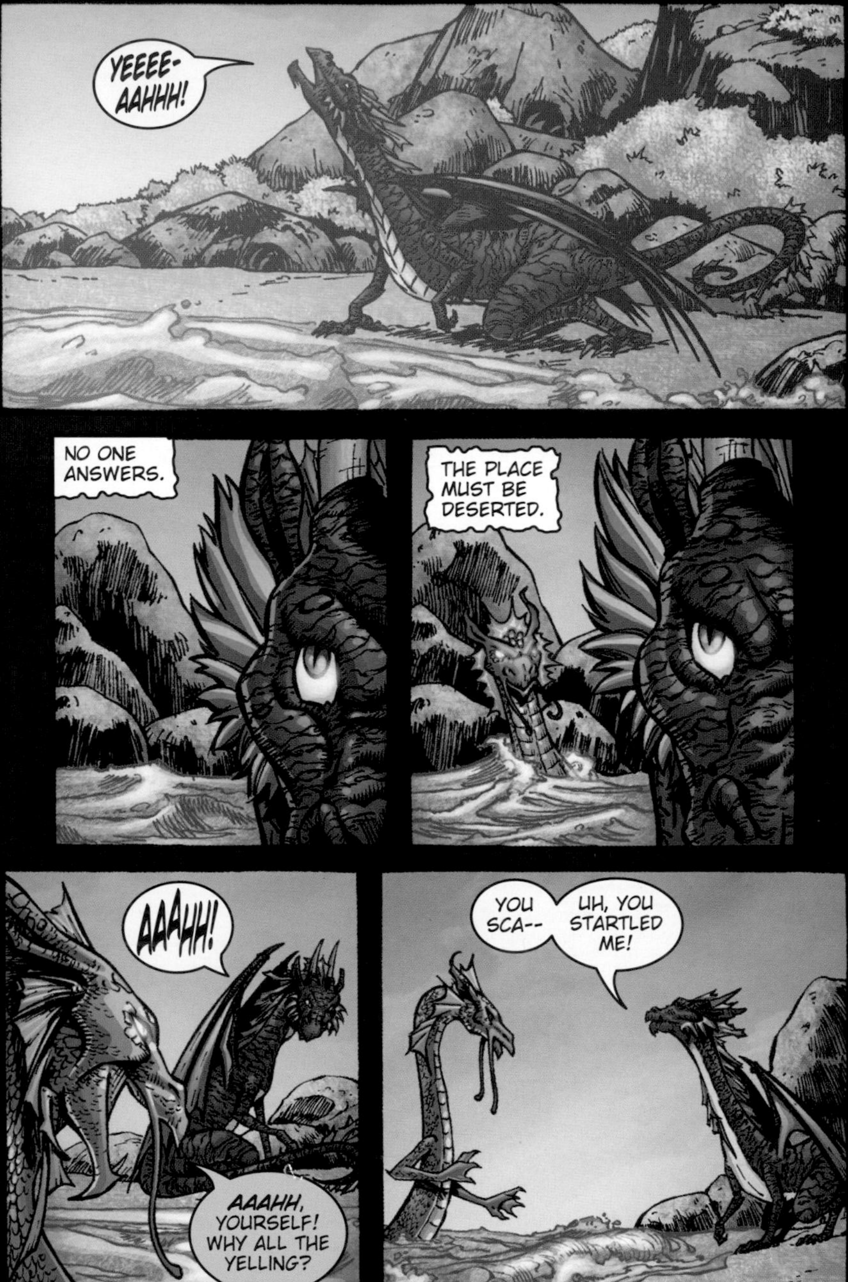
YEEEE-
AAHHH!
NO ONE ANSWERS.
THE PLACE MUST BE DESERTED.
AAAHH!
AAAHH, YOURSELF! WHY ALL THE YELLING?
YOU SCA--
UH, YOU STARTLED ME!

GO ON TO THE NEXT PAGE.

"Sorry," says the strange monster from the sea. It looks a lot like a dragon but with webbed feet and no wings. "I was just fishing in the shallow water here, when I heard you making all that noise."

"Oh," you answer. "Well, I was hoping to find . . . somebody like myself."

"Then you're too late," the sea monster says. "There *was* a dragon here. But she left a day or two ago."

You were so close to finding another dragon! "Which way did she go?" you ask eagerly.

The monster flaps his finny foreleg in the direction of your home. "She headed toward the sunrise," it says. "She said something about a lot of treasure hidden in a mountain."

You stare in surprise. "You mean *my* treasure?" You left it unguarded!

GO ON TO THE NEXT PAGE.

"I don't know about *your* treasure, but the other dragon did leave some around," says the sea monster. "See that big cave over there?" it asks, pointing. "The seabirds say it's full of shiny stuff."

You thank the creature and dart quickly to the cave. The opening is more than large enough for you, and once you get inside, the cave is warm and dry. A little farther in, you find the hoard the other dragon left behind. It's not quite as large as your own, but there are all sorts of new, interesting objects—glittering machines with crystal gears. It's a nice trade. And you have your favorite thing, your clock, anyway.

You climb your new pile of gold and place your clock at the very top. It will take you years to examine every one of your new treasures. What an incredible birthday present—even if it was a few days late!

THE END

YOU'LL GIVE THE KNIGHT A BIG SURPRISE!
HE HASN'T SEEN YOU YET...
NOW HE'S DONE IT...
HE TOUCHED YOUR TREASURE!
ROARRR
CLANK
CLASH
GRRR!!!

TWISTED JOURNEYS®

It's been some time since you
fought a knight. This one is strong.

WILL YOU . . .

. . . keep fighting?

TURN TO PAGE 30.

. . . try to get away?

TURN TO PAGE 38.

You hear shouts of amazement from the sailors below as you burn their arrows right out of the sky. You dive toward the largest ship, which has a flag flying from the top of a tall, wooden pole—the mast, you think it's called. You burn the flag into flaming tatters.

Most of the men scramble for places to hide, but a few stay out in plain sight. These men are armed like knights, with swords, but they have no shields. You plunge straight toward them, bellowing. The fire rises from deep in your chest and flows out, blasting the men in front of you.

As the sun sets, the city is lit up by the flames of the ships you have set on fire. Anyone could see that from miles and miles away. If another dragon lived nearby, surely he would have appeared by now.

Disappointed, you fly away into the night. Surely, the people here will tell stories about you for many generations. And you have the entire rest of the world to search for others of your kind.

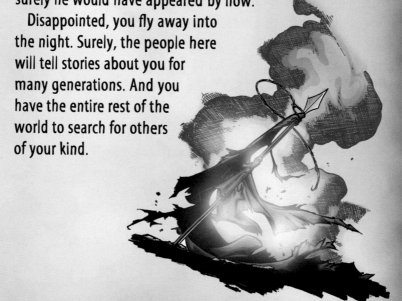

THE END

You jump into the air and hover over the hilltop. "I'm tired of waiting," you roar. "Find your own way home, if you can."

"Wait!" the old woman calls. "I've found what I was searching for." She turns toward you, holding a large stone jar in both hands. She waits as you slowly lower yourself back down to the hilltop.

"This drink will make you breathe fire," she says.

"Grandmother . . ." the girl starts to say.

"Hush, child," says the old woman. She pours the jar's contents into a bowl formed by one of the broken rocks.

It's such a small sip . . . could that work? You stick your head forward and lap it up quickly as you watch the old woman out of the corner of your eye. The liquid is thick and burns your throat. It burns your stomach. It burns . . . everything.

In a way, the old woman told the truth. As you fall to the ground, your insides are on fire, and your breath is hot as flame.

THE END

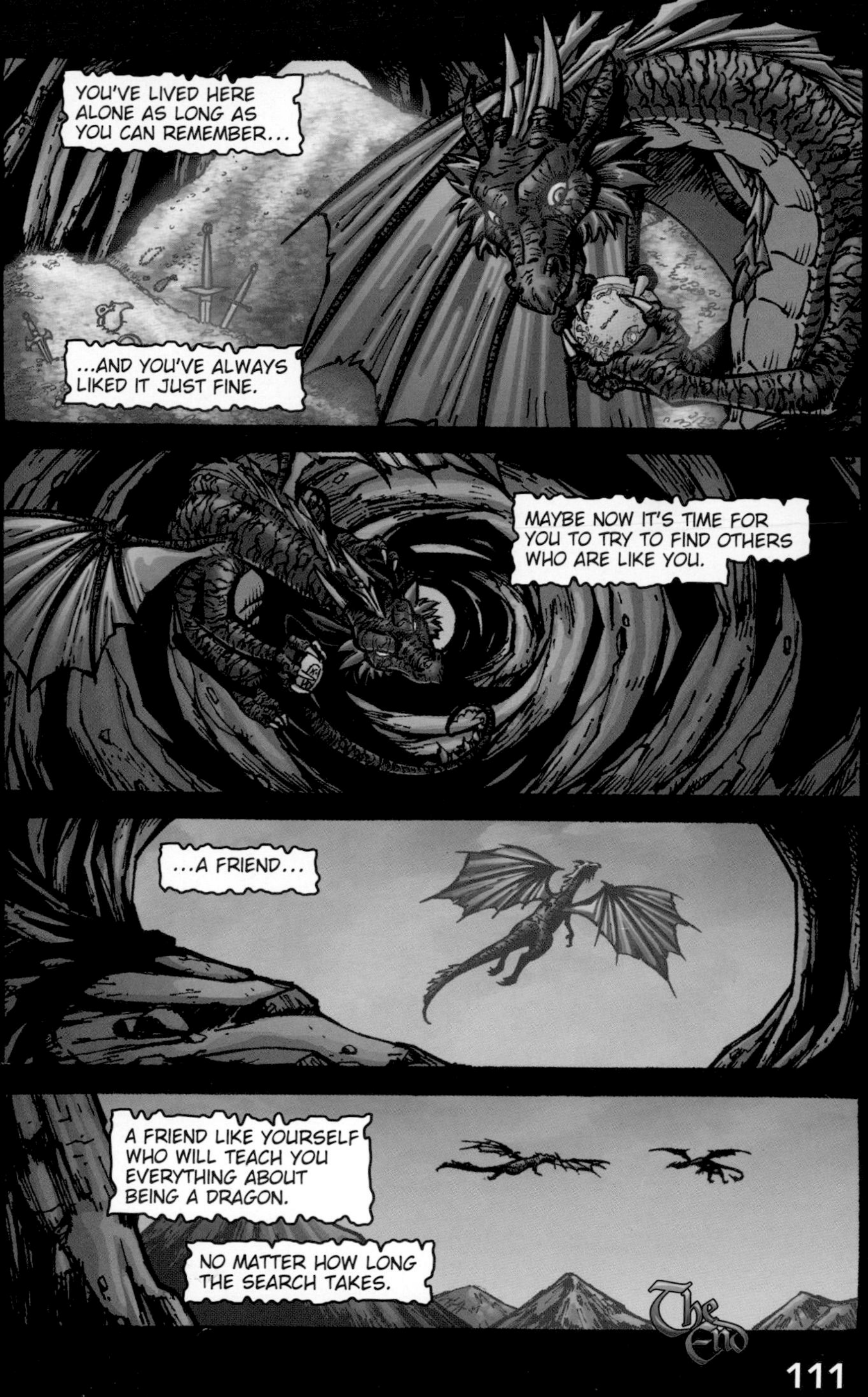
YOU'VE LIVED HERE ALONE AS LONG AS YOU CAN REMEMBER...
...AND YOU'VE ALWAYS LIKED IT JUST FINE.
MAYBE NOW IT'S TIME FOR YOU TO TRY TO FIND OTHERS WHO ARE LIKE YOU.
...A FRIEND...
A FRIEND LIKE YOURSELF WHO WILL TEACH YOU EVERYTHING ABOUT BEING A DRAGON.
NO MATTER HOW LONG THE SEARCH TAKES.
The End

EXPERIENCE ALL OF THE
TWISTED JOURNEYS®

#1 CAPTURED BY PIRATES
Will these scurvy pirates turn you into
shark bait?

#2 ESCAPE FROM PYRAMID X
Not every ancient mummy stays dead . . .

#3 TERROR IN GHOST MANSION
The spooks in this Halloween house aren't
wearing costumes . . .

#4 THE TREASURE OF MOUNT FATE
Can you survive monsters and magic and
bring home the treasure?

#5 NIGHTMARE ON ZOMBIE ISLAND
Will you be the first to escape Zombie Island?

#6 THE TIME TRAVEL TRAP
Danger is everywhere when you're caught
in a time machine!

#7 VAMPIRE HUNT
These vampire hunters are hunting for *you!*

#8 ALIEN INCIDENT ON PLANET J
Make peace with the aliens, or you'll
never get off their planet . . .

**#9 AGENT MONGOOSE AND THE
HYPNO-BEAM SCHEME**
Your top-secret mission: foil the plots of
an evil mastermind!

#10 THE GOBLIN KING
Will you join the fearsome goblins or
the dangerous elves?

#11 SHIPWRECKED ON MAD ISLAND
Mad scientists and mutants are on your trail!

#12 KUNG FU MASTERS
Can you master kung fu in time to battle
bandits and ghosts?

#13 SCHOOL OF EVIL
The teachers are creepy, monsters lurk in
the lab, and your dorm room is haunted!

#14 ATTACK OF THE MUTANT METEORS
Can you survive being sky-tall or bug-small?

**#15 AGENT MONGOOSE AND THE
ATTACK OF THE GIANT INSECTS**
Your top-secret mission: squash a bug invasion!

#16 THE QUEST FOR DRAGON MOUNTAIN
Will you hoard gold or seek adventure? You're
the dragon, you decide!